Falling Pleasures

Sexy Stories Collection

VOLUME 30

10 EROTIC SHORT STORIES

MACKENZIE HARNDEN

Publisher's Note: This is a work of fiction. Names, characters, places, and incidents are a product of the author's imagination. Locales and public names are sometimes used for atmospheric purposes. Any resemblance to actual people, living or dead, or to businesses, companies, events, institutions, or locales is completely coincidental.

Falling Pleasures/ Mackenzie Harnden. -- 1st ed.
Xplicit Press, an imprint of TLM Media LLC

ISBN-13: 978-1-62327-561-7
ISBN-10: 1-62327-561-X
eISBN: 978-1-62327-611-9

Printed in the United States of America

CONTENTS

1 STRETCH PART 1

Stretch had acquired his name for very practical and logical reasons. A laboratory accident combined with a natural genetic mutation had given him the ability to alter his molecular structure. Because of this, he could change the shape of his body parts, making them appear longer, shorter, fatter, thinner, and otherwise completely different. He could not alter his mass; he could make it appear so by altering his basic molecular structure.

Over the years, Stretch had learned to use his freaky talent to his advantage, including in seducing women. Tonight, Stretch had gone for his prize: a leggy dark blonde model with huge baby-blue eyes that fluttered their oversized lashes in his direction every opportunity they got. Stretch wasn't the most handsome among the men at the annual celebration ball, but he sure was the most noticeable. Stretch embraced his differences and went to extreme measures to express them, making him appear very eccentric. Tonight, Stretch donned a cream ruffled tuxedo accompanied by a pale-blue silk shirt and bow tie to match, making him stand out among the black-and-white sea of penguin suits that surrounded him.

He pretended to be uninterested in the blonde who flashed looks in his way, increasing her intent with each glance. He appeared not to notice. He continued to engage in conversation with the group of well-to-do middle-aged men that surrounded him until one by one, they left for the buffet and he was left standing next to one of his best friends. He leant over and discreetly whispered in his ear.

"You clocked the ole blondie-legs-eleven over there?"

"Who hasn't," his friend replied, "whoooooooo, what I wouldn't give."

"I bet she's a right taker."

Stretch had an edge of smugness in his voice. He looked the blonde up and down once again, this time with more due care and attention. He started with her feet and noticed that she wore killer heels that must have added five inches or so to her legs, but even without this secret weapon, she would still be tall enough to look him directly in the eye and wrap those luscious legs around him three times over. Stretch couldn't wait to wrap his around her. He worked his way up her long lean legs. They were pale and he could tell she had used shimmer; they glinted in the soft lighting of the function room. Her ankles were delicate and slender, and her calves were well shaped and toned. As he worked his eyes up her thighs, he felt his arousal rise as he noticed the defined feminine curves of her muscular, athletic structure.

"I intend to find out."

He wandered over to the buffet, which just happened to be behind the blonde woman. He would have to cross her path to get there. She would have to notice him not noticing her again; he wanted to make sure he had her full attention before he attempted to make his move.

As Stretch strutted past her, he made sure not to pay her any attention that she would be aware of, yet clocked the rest of her glorious body as he swept by. Her dress was short, black, and very revealing. It skimmed just below her bottom and Stretch found himself wondering whether she was wearing underwear or not. In his imagination, she wasn't, and he unzipped himself there and then, bent her over the buffet table, and stuck his massive throbbing member inside her, but that was only his imagination; those sorts of antics would have to wait.

The dress was figure-hugging, and boy did she have a figure. He was viewing her from behind properly for the first time. She had a heavenly behind—not too much junk in the trunk but enough to give her that gorgeous curvaceous shape. He imagined himself caressing her wobbling buttocks as he pounded her from behind. She'd love it, he thought to himself. Her curves were emphasized by her tiny waist. It looked small enough for him to be able to get both his hands around it. Her dress showcased it perfectly. As Stretch swept back round to her front, he noticed her arms and shoulders were bare and her neckline was plunging. She had a cleavage that would leave even the likes of Monroe and Mansfield green with envy. They were huge, natural, and perfectly formed. How she held them in there he did not know, but he couldn't wait to help her get them out. They looked amazing. He imagined himself burying his face in them as he bounced her naked body up and down on him. Her pale complexion gleamed under the soft lighting, emphasized by the shimmer, and Stretch couldn't wait to get his hands on all of her.

He reached the buffet table and heard the telltale clip, clop of killer heels on wooden flooring behind him. She had noticed him and her patience had waned. He felt her approach him and watched her appear by his side out of the corner of his eye.

"You know it's rude to stare, and it's even ruder to then go out of your way to ignore the person you're staring at."

She flashed her captivating white smile to him, with two rows of perfect teeth, surrounded by full red lips. Stretch was lost for words. Up close her beauty was even more mesmerizing.

"You can close your mouth now; the goldfish look doesn't become you."

She reached up and pressed his bottom jaw closed with her middle finger as she turned her back on the table, still not looking at him.

"I don't know about you, but there's only one thing my appetite hungers for at this table," she licked her lips as she smirked and inspected her wineglass very carefully. "And it isn't the food or fine wine," she smirked.

Stretch recognized his opportune moment and slid along the table closer beside her.

"I think everyone else is hungry for the same thing, and I'd be glad to feed you your desires."

He spoke softly near her ear so the others couldn't hear. He slid his near arm round her waist and squeezed her buttocks, she gently pushed them back in to his hand, and he felt the bottom of her dress, just reaching the edge of the table. He quickly scanned the room to make sure he wasn't being watched by the wrong people and decided to satisfy his curiosity. He reached under it and found, to his delight, that his imagination had served him well: he could find no trace of underwear. He even stroked between the crevice of her upper thighs where it met her hot wet lips and slipped a cheeky finger inside her; she released a tiny gasp, and he expanded it inside her.

"Until you're so full, you're bursting for more."

He felt his arousal strain against his trousers and concentrated on adjusting its size so she wouldn't notice.

She hastily moved away to face him, making sure she was maintaining her dignity, and she discreetly pulled her dress down. Despite the briefness of the contact, his antics had left her sodden. She looked him in the eye, which she noticed, stared at her cleavage, and told him, "Meet me upstairs in three minutes; a moment longer and I'll sort myself out."

Stretch raised an eyebrow and wore a bewildered expression; she must be taking the piss, he thought to himself. She leant forward and whispered in his ear.

"I know who you are, Stretch, and I want to find out for myself if you live up to your reputation."

Stretch was gobsmacked; he knew his reputation preceded him, but he didn't realize just how much. This had never happened before—never with a woman as beautiful as this. He felt himself blush with a mixture of excitement, embarrassment, and, most of all, anxiety. He hoped he lived up to her expectations as well; never had he felt such pressure to perform. He was determined to give the hot, leggy blonde a night she would never forget. She sauntered off, and as he watched her hips swing from side to side with her panty-less arse following it, he couldn't believe his luck. Stretch leant with his back against the table and glanced up at the clock. He felt himself grow harder as he imagined what was about to transpire and concentrated on adjusting his size so that no one noticed. He smiled to himself. He grew to love his ability more and more as each day passed; there was very little he couldn't do now that he'd mastered it. He gave another glance at the clock—time to go. He swept the floor with his eyes clocking the remaining guests and those who were watching—no one important; he was off.

He heard her before he saw her; she made delicate little whimpers of pleasure that guided him. He knew he was late, and she knew he wanted to be. He opened the door of the red room upstairs to find her sitting on a chair with her legs spread, stoking her swollen expectant clitoris. She paused and looked up as she heard him approach.

"Why, come in," she told him.

"I intend to. May I join in with the party?" She knew the question was rhetorical. She flashed him a dirty smirk.

"Only if you can get to it from where you already are." Stretch took this as an open invitation, for it certainly wasn't a challenge.

"Very well, as you wish, milady."

He extended his small finger towards her and noticed that she stopped what she was doing as she watched his little finger get longer. First, a foot, then two, then three, then, it was there, rubbing against her already excited clitoris as dexterous and nimble as if he were right there in front of her. She released a sigh of pleasure.

"Oh, my!" she exclaimed. "That is quite a talent," she said beneath pleasurable sighs as her excitement grew. Stretch cocked his head to one side and flashed a dirty half smirk. His confidence grew.

"That's just the beginning," and he poked his tongue out and reached towards her.

Stretch slid his finger down to her moist, vacant hole and slid his little finger inside it and flicked her clitoris with his tongue. Her sighs turned to delicate little whimpers once more, indicating he was nearer the spot now. He extended another finger towards her and slipped it inside her.

"Oh yes, more," she demanded, writhing on him with her head tilted back. Stretch moved his fingers up and down inside her using his ability; his wrist and the pressure he used on her remained firm and constant. He slipped another finger inside her and expanded it as he felt her insides ripen with anticipation. She pushed herself against him as he brought her closer to climax.

"More tongue," she demanded. Stretch obeyed and flattened and widened his tongue against her so that it resembled that of animals and lapped it fast and furious over her swollen clitoris.

"Oh yes," she squealed, and he felt her clench down on him, gushing her juices everywhere as she came. Wow, a squirter; he felt his excitement increase and took one stride to cross the room to reach her.

"My turn," she jumped forward and ripped his pants and underwear down off him. What she saw was not what she expected—he was tiny.

"No, it was just to be discreet. Keep watching," he told her, almost panicking at his precautionary mistake. They both stared as they observed his penis grow before them. First, six inches, then seven, then eight, then...."

"Whoa, that's enough," she told him and reached forward, licking up and down his shaft as she cupped his balls in her soft, delicate hands. She caressed them so gently he felt a tingling sensation course through his entire body and back down into his penis. She took it in his mouth and began to suck on it. Feeling unable to contain himself, Stretch pulled her to her feet and ripped her dress off, revealing the full splendor of her hot body, as he drank it in with his eyes; he almost exploded there and then. Everything about her was perfectly proportioned and complemented her. Her blonde hair, pale skin, baby-blue eyes, and curvaceous figure were a delight to anyone's eyes, and he couldn't get enough of it. She noticed how he enjoyed looking at her and gave him a twirl. Her behind was even better; she gave him a little show, reaching her arms up above her head, whipping her hair, and wiggling her hips and buttocks from side to side.

Stretch's imagination was running wild; here she was flaunting herself at him, practically begging him to take her, and he obliged.

She bent over and Stretch slammed himself inside her from where he was. She screamed and pushed back, and he withdrew again.

"Is that all you've got?" she glanced back at him. Stretch grabbed hold of her buttocks and pulled her towards him; she leant flat back over the chair as he slammed himself inside her again and again, increasing his size with each thrust. He watched as his sides reached her limit and strained against them, pulling her apart. She screamed with pleasure as she felt him grow deeper and wider inside her. As he grew past what she could naturally accommodate, she spread her legs wider in response and pushed back on him harder.

"Oh yes, more," she demanded again. Stretch leant over her and reached down with his tongue, licking between her labia until he found her clitoris.

"Fuck yes," she screamed as he made contact. He felt her increase the pace of her motion as she continued to push back against his hard and fast slams, and as he brought her to another screaming climax, he felt her hot, wet juices gush all over his hot and throbbing penis. The clenching of her walls brought him to an intense and satisfying climax. She felt the warmth of his release fill her and pulled away from him.

He sat in the chair to recover and noticed she was sprawled on the crimson sheets of the red room's bed on her side. He'd never witnessed such a sexy woman who wanted him so much in all his life, despite his ability, and then he was there again.

"Fancy joining me," she winked, rubbing the sheet with one hand and herself with the other.

"My pleasure," Stretch took one step to reach the bed on the other side of the room. He was lying next to her and heard her gasp as he slid his finger inside her. He leant forward and kissed her, and she was amazed to feel his tongue explore untouched places she had never been aware of before. He stimulated sensations inside that she didn't even know existed. She couldn't control herself from writhing and moaning, her hands wandering all over him, demanding more.

Stretch maneuvered her so that her legs dangled over the edge of the bed; he slid off himself, knelt down before her, and spread them. He plunged inside her with his tongue and used his middle finger to slide over her clitoris, not actually moving his hand or finger at all but just rapidly extending its length back and forth over her swollen clitoris. She felt him move and expand his tongue deeper inside her as he whirled it around, filling her depths and expanding them as far as they would go. She felt him hitting her G-spot—and every other spot of the alphabet inside her. She was sure that twenty-six letters just weren't enough to cover them all. Just as she felt herself about to come, Stretch withdrew and exchanged his finger for his tongue, and vice versa.

"Mmmmmmmm, so close," she gasped through gritted teeth as she continued to writhe. Stretch removed his little finger and inserted his thumb, extending it so that it reached the bottom of her cavernous depths. He felt her walls start to throb as he rubbed the tip over them.

"That any better?" she continued to vocalize her satisfied response.

"Fuck yes, make it bigger," she demanded. Stretch increased the size of his thumb until it was almost the size of an average penis. The extra movement and control he had over his thumb in comparison brought her to a series of intense multiple orgasms. As he felt her sodden genitals relax further, he took his entire fist, shrank it down to half of its size, and thrust it inside her. She threw herself back, screamed, and writhed over it; she felt him extend the tips of his fingers inside her to tickle her depths. He felt her relax further into herself, and he plunged and expanded his fist, thrusting it in and out using his ability to make her come harder and faster with each stroke. She grabbed his head between her legs in a vice-like grip that would have suffocated him had he not readjusted the shape of his head to accommodate for his breathing. Lucky she was too involved in what he was doing to her to notice; otherwise, she would have had quite a fright if she'd looked up. The sheets were soon soaked and his face felt as though he'd just had a shower.

"Take me now!" she demanded as he stood up and grabbed him round the hips with her thighs, wrapping her legs around him and guiding him down into her. Stretch expanded deep inside her. He thrust in and out of her, and she began to wail with pleasure and begged him for more as he brought her to climax over and over again. He leant over and reached down with his tongue to heighten the sensation and slipped it inside of her as well to add extra lubrication as he expanded his girth until she was about to burst. She reached down to grab hold of it and found she was unable to fit her hand around him and felt him grow even bigger under her touch. The growth strained against her and she felt it pull her legs wider apart. The sensation felt so intense she howled and pushed herself down onto him, begging him to fuck her harder and faster than he'd ever fucked any woman before her.

Stretch whipped her round onto all fours while still inside her and pounded her hard and fast from behind, leaning back to admire the magnificent view. He reached under with fingers, thumbs, and his tongue to intensify her orgasmic pleasure and watched her juices dripping down her and all over him. He'd never felt this aroused fucking a woman whose name he didn't even know nor care about. He was just making sure he remembered and enjoyed every last moment of this glorious ecstasy. She pushed back on him harder and faster as he continued to drive himself deeper inside her. Her legs were spread as wide as they could go, and he was sure she would be walking like John Wayne tomorrow, and he smiled to himself. He felt his excitement rise one last time and reach its peak, and he cried out as he exploded inside of her. She clenched her walls and pushed back in response, crying out as she did so. She collapsed forward onto the bed once she was done. Stretch lay beside her.

"So, disappointed?" Stretch asked her. She smiled at him as she raised her buttocks into the air, post-coital fluid leaking from her spent vagina, and she maneuvered herself off the bed. Stretch attempted to follow her but found that he was unable to move. He looked up to find his hands bound so tight it would take him a good few minutes to shrink them out. He looked back at the leggy blonde, now with her dress back on and her hair arranged perfectly.

"Hey, what the...," he began but she placed a finger on his lips to shush him as she straddled him and whispered in his ear.

"You do realize that all your other body parts go floppy while you're horny?"

His mouth dropped and his eyes widened as he stared at her with a shocked expression.

"Yes, Stretch, even you have a weakness. It just took a while to figure it out."

She looked honest and sincere, not at all sinister, as she stroked back a stray lock of his hair. What is this woman about?, he wondered; he couldn't figure out what she wanted from him, other than the obvious, but was that just a mask for a deeper, underlying purpose?

"There's plenty more where that came from, but you're through to round two. Until next time. Goodbye."

And with that, she was gone.

It took Stretch a good few minutes to

manipulate the shape of his hands enough to free himself from the ropes she had used to tie him with. He couldn't figure out how she'd managed to bind him like that without him noticing. He pondered about what she'd told him about his weakness and her final words. What could they mean? He wondered. Well, he was sure of one thing: there was only one way to find out the answers. He'd have to participate in these activities with her again, but when? And who was she? This mysterious exotic blonde beauty he'd never seen before in his life, and what did she want from him?

2 STRETCH PART 2

It had been over three months since Stretch had his encounter with the sensational blonde woman. Not a day had passed where he hadn't thought about her. But he hadn't seen her again. Stretch hadn't seen so much as a glimpse of her. He was beginning to feel that she had just been playing games with him. Her words had had quite an impact at the time; he always thought he was so careful regarding his weaknesses. She'd played him like a pawn that night.

One wet October night as Stretch left work, she appeared out of nowhere. As he passed an alleyway, he heard a pssst in his ear and felt a gentle tap on his shoulder. Startled, he whipped round and came face to face with her. Before he could utter a sound, she pressed her finger to his lips, leaned in closed, and said to him, "Follow me. It's important."

Stretch did as he was told and found himself wandering down an alley he had been careful to avoid for years. Although he was more than capable of looking after himself, he knew that the alley had a reputation. In fact, less than a week ago, one of his work colleagues had been mugged in the same alley. The thieves had pulled him into it and threatened him with a gun, all for the pieces of paper in his wallet. He escaped unhurt but was shaken.

Stretch felt anxious as she walked down the alley. It was dark and uninviting and smelled of stale beer and rotting food. He wondered what on Earth she wanted from him here of all places. He began to question her motives and wondered what she may be hiding under the large black coat she was wearing. Had she brought him here only to pull a gun on him? His fear increased as he felt her suddenly push him against the wall. He instinctively raised his hands in surrender, expecting this to be his last breath. He shut his eyes and was surprised to feel her lips pressed against his. She took his hands and guided them down over her face and pressed them against her cleavage. She pushed herself against him and felt him swell against her. Stretch relaxed and didn't even attempt to disguise the arousal he was now feeling.

She unzipped his trousers and exposed him. He slid his hands under her coat and found she was naked. Stretch had never felt such sexual excitement in all his life. He reached down and felt that she was already wet. He was sure there were other people around, but he didn't care and neither did she.

"Take me now," she demanded, shoving two of his fingers inside her.

"My pleasure," he replied as he extended his member and shaped it so that it slid into her, spreading her legs apart as it did. She gasped in his ear as he entered her and pushed down on him. He felt a wet gush leaking all over him. Without moving his body, he thrust his extended penis in and out of her, feeling her push back down and against him in response. She moaned in his ear. He grasped and felt her wonderful cleavage and felt it spill over his hands as he fought to contain them. He expanded his hands so he could enjoy feeling it wobble within his grasp as she moved up and down on him.

"Mmmm, touch me," she demanded and grabbed his tongue between her fingertips. She pulled it from his mouth and guided it down to her clitoris, tilting her hips and guiding him to the swollen and expectant nodule. She let out a slight squeal as he made contact. He flicked it over her and felt her jerk in response. She could feel herself reaching her peak as he continued to stimulate her.

"I want to feel more of you."

Stretch responded in kind by expanding his penis until he felt her walls strain against him.

"Oh yes," she shrieked as she writhed against him. He lapped over her sodden genitals and brought her to an intense and dripping orgasm. She felt herself clench over him as she came and the sensation rose up within her. Stretch felt the release wash through him as she clenched over him and grunted as he finished with her. They leaned against one another for a moment in the alleyway, both now eager for more. She smiled up at him.

"Now, pull us up, up, and away."

"Huh?"

Stretch was confused. She pointed above her; there were several fire escapes and other solid objects protruding from the tower block buildings above him.

"It's not safe here now. Pull us up."

She wrapped her arms and legs around

him with him still inside her.

"You do realize I don't have superstrength?" She smiled and nodded.

"How insulting. I'm not that heavy. Try it."

Stretch sighed with frustration. He didn't want to feel emasculated if he couldn't lift both of them up, neither did he want to disappoint her. He looked up at the options above him.

"Anywhere particular in mind?"

"Just up."

He reached above him and grasped on the nearest fire escape. Using his ability, he pushed up with his legs and pulled with his arms; it was a lot of effort and sweat rolled down his brow, but he managed to get them both up to the first level.

"Good, now try the rooftop."

Stretch looked at her, disgruntled.

"Would you mind telling me why you want us to keep going up?"

"I'll explain all when we get to the rooftop. Now, up."

Feeling more confident and still inside the beautiful blonde woman, Stretch reached and pushed up until they reached the rooftop. He set her down and watched his cum flow out of her as he did so. She felt the warm trickle run down her leg, and she wiped it with her hand and licked it off. She stared deep into his eyes as she did so.

He felt aroused again as he hung over the side of the building, drawing his legs up and all of himself over the edge of the building on to the rooftop. He crawled away from it and lay down to recover. His manhood protruded erect and wanting from his trousers. The blonde woman sauntered over to him and straddled him. She sat down hard on his penis and began bouncing on top of him, squealing with pleasure. Stretch didn't question her actions and went with the flow, guiding her up and down on him over and over.

She stood up and moved down and took him in her mouth. Stretch released a gasp of pleasure as he watched her. He felt her stimulate him with her tongue and cup his balls. The pleasure rose from deep within him. He wanted to get his hands all over her as he enjoyed feeling her pleasure him, so he extended them down beside him. He reached over her back and pressed firmly as he stroked his hands down over her spine down to her buttocks, which he caressed and spanked when he got there. She wriggled in response and pushed back against him, still sucking and stroking him with her mouth. He reached his hands to the crevice of her buttocks. With one hand, he placed a finger inside her and, with the other, reached underneath her and found her swollen and expectant clitoris waiting for him. She moaned as he made contact and the vibrations caused waves of pleasure to shoot up through him. He gasped.

He moved his finger in and out of her vigorously and felt her grow wetter. He expanded his finger, gradually filling her up. The more he filled her, the noisier she became until the vibrations became so intense; Stretch felt the hot rush rise within and out of him, filling her throat as he released inside her mouth. He felt her walls contract hard over his finger as he brought her to a finish at the same time.

Stretch extended his penis down and penetrated her from behind; he watched with pleasure as she gasped and pushed back on him. He had the pleasure of lying down in comfort while he watched himself fuck her doggy style, with a front view. He considered changing to rear view half way through. She screamed and writhed in pleasure as he inserted his penis in and out of her and stimulated her clitoris with his finger. She rose to her knees and pushed back on him hard; he expanded himself inside her and she spread her legs to accommodate his massive member. He admired the glorious view. Her breasts bounced but remained perky and perfectly formed; he enjoyed watching her caress them herself as she bounced up and down on him. He admired her beautifully toned torso and abs and the glorious curves of her hips and muscular, toned thighs. She looked even more sensational than he remembered. He felt his stimulation increase and the rise of another climax growing within him.

He shifted his position so he could now see her from behind. She just continued to writhe and bounce, squirting her orgasmic juices all over him. The view from behind was just as spectacular. He watched beads of sweat roll down her spine. Her tiny waist accentuated the beautiful curves and crevices formed by her pert toned bottom, which jiggled in rhythm to her writhes and his thrusts. He let the sensation wash over him and released yet again inside her. She responded in kind and clenched her walls over him harder than ever, screaming as she jerked and squirted all over him in a spectacular climactic finish. Stretch wondered if anyone was able to hear them up here or if this was the most private place to fuck ever. Either way, there was something about fucking the sensational blonde woman, whose name he did not know, up here on the rooftops that just got him started all over again. He leaned over her and continued to fuck her, expanding as much as he could inside her until she felt tighter than a wound-up clock and until they both reach another intense climax.

"Stop," she demanded this time.

"Why?" Stretch asked, now feeling annoyed. "And why on Earth have you brought me up here? What's going on?"

"They're after you," she told him.

"What the, who? What the hell are you on about, woman?"

"My name is Kirsty; I work for the government. That's all you need to know."

"I don't understand, they're already protecting me, and I can look after myself. I'm damn sure of that now."

"You have no idea what you are capable of, and neither do they. We need to go now. You must come with me. If they get hold of you, it won't just be you who's in danger."

Kirsty strode away to the edge of the building and leaped across to the adjacent rooftop. It wasn't very far and Stretch stepped across barely using his ability.

"We may need your ability in a moment the gaps widen," she called to him.

"Would you at least tell me where we're going, please?"

"I can't. It's too dangerous."

Stretch rolled his eyes in frustration, but accepted he was just wasting his energy. He and Kirsty leapt from rooftop to rooftop for what felt like hours. Sometimes Stretch needed to use his ability to stride over while he carried her. They reached an old moss-covered rooftop that appeared to need some attention, as cracks were appearing that he was sure would lead to leaking of the roof below, and it was here where Kirsty stopped.

She opened a well-disguised hatch that was camouflaged by the moss that had grown over it. They entered the building. She jumped Stretch in the stairwell and he took her there and then again. He slipped her coat off her shoulders, revealing her beautiful naked body, and this time she tore his clothes, ripping them from him. Her eyes and hands wandered together over the definition of his muscles; he had a great body, and she enjoyed admiring it for a change. She licked her lips as she traced her fingers down over his defined chest to his well-pronounced abs. Watching her become turned on at the sight of him overcame him, and he pulled her towards him, wrapping his arms around. They buried their faces in each other in a tantalizing kiss that sent shock waves coursing through them both. Stretch pulled back and looked deep into her gorgeous baby-blue eyes.

"I've never wanted a woman as much as I do you. You're truly mesmerizing."

A smile spread across her face as he said it, and she placed her hands behind his head and pulled him towards her, taking his lips in her full ones, sucking on them until they swelled and tingled like hers did below. She felt Stretch's hands roving all over her body. Caressing her neck, stroking down her spine and round across her collarbone, down to her chest, he expanded his already large hands to accommodate all of her cleavage, then down her flat, toned tummy, over the luscious curves of her hips, and round behind her.

He tucked his hands between her cheeks and stroked her buttocks, parting her legs slightly, then he worked his way under her thighs and eventually found her wet hot swollen mound and her wet, dripping vagina, both expectant and anticipating his every move. She enjoyed feeling the tingling sensations dart about through her body, following the warm trail of touch on her skin his hands left behind. As he found her hot, wet, and dripping, she spread her legs and leaned in towards him, planting another hungry kiss on his eager pout.

Stretch's kiss was filled with passion and great technique and left her yearning for more. She pressed harder against his mouth and let her tongue slide inside to find his. He rubbed over her clitoris harder and faster with his expanding finger, inserting another one inside her. Kirsty felt the telltale stirrings of a tingle deep within her, indicating that her climax was coming. She gasped as the sensation increased, growing with every stroke. She felt his normal-sized manhood protruding against her, eager to penetrate her and fill her depths. She reached for it with her hand and rubbed it over the length of his shaft; she heard him sigh and felt him relax into her, increasing his pace on her as he did so. Kirsty couldn't help but release a small squeal no matter how hard she tried to contain it. Stretch felt her depths expand, ready to accommodate him, and her juices release to aid him deep down inside her. Kirsty was almost there and writhed over his now penis-sized finger, pushing against him and leaning all of her bodyweight onto him as she reached an intense and satisfying orgasm.

Stretch knew she had just cum. He couldn't hold back any longer. He knelt down ever so slightly so he could get a good natural momentum. Despite his ability, he still enjoyed a good bit of old-fashioned thrusting, and he hadn't had the opportunity to do so in a while. So he angled his body and slid himself inside with the aid of her guidance. She moaned and sat down hard on him as he did so and he grunted his response. He pushed hard against her and felt her jump up a bit and wrap her legs around him behind his head. He was impressed at her agility and grabbed hold of them to stabilize her. He felt her depths expand and let his penis do the same to fill them. Kirsty moaned as she felt Stretch's penis growing inside her, the sensation stimulated her walls to start contracting every time. She felt herself respond internally and vocalized her pleasure as it rushed up and overcame her. She felt Stretch thrusting her back in to the cold hard wall over and over with great force. He hadn't fucked her hard yet and she was enjoying every second.

A moment of sadness washed over her as she realized it couldn't last. Then the feeling of climax overcame her and she screamed and clenched down hard on his penis. He slammed her back in to the wall and expanded himself further inside her with a grunt. She spread her legs wider to accommodate him and did her best to bounce up and down over him, making shrill sounds of pleasure as he brought her to another round of orgasms. He grabbed hold of her elegant, slender hands and clasped them in his broad and masculine ones. He pinned them against the wall above her head and pinned her body there with his penis. Fast and furious, he slammed himself in and out of her harder and faster than ever. He thrust with all his body and used his ability to penetrate her as deep as he could without hurting her. Kirsty lay upright against the wall and arched her back to get the best angle to accommodate as much of him inside her as possible.

Stretch looked down and saw her dripping all over his massive manhood; he could feel the hot juices leaking from her and pouring continuously over him, and he wanted to taste them. He reached down with his tongue and began lapping her up. Kirsty's moans grew louder and more intense in harmony with the sensation of her orgasms. She felt lost in this moment with Stretch who felt the intensity rise along his hot, throbbing shaft. He couldn't hold back any longer. He sped up his thrusts and penetrated her deeper than ever, slamming himself harder and faster inside her. Kirsty's pleasurable response finished him off, and as he felt her clench down hard and writhe all over him, he exploded inside her and cried out in ecstasy.

As they finished, Kirsty smiled and told him, "You're safe now; they can't get you here," then the world went black.

3 FALLING PART 1

Matthew and Shelly met six weeks ago. They hit it off straight away and have been going on dates ever since. Tonight, Matthew planned to ask Shelly to be his girlfriend. He had liked her since he had first laid eyes on her, but he couldn't find the right way to tell her. Instead, he decided to show her; he knew she liked to star gaze and often missed the countryside now that she was living in a city. He decided he would take her to a beautiful spot a few miles out of town that he knew was quite popular with couples his age and ask her at the right moment.

Shelly had also liked Matthew from the moment they met; she couldn't get enough of looking in to his endearing eyes. She was aware that they had been dating a few weeks now and they hadn't slept together, and he hadn't asked her to be his girlfriend, yet. She hoped he would soon.

Matthew and Shelly felt as though they were falling for one another, fast. They were both happy to take things slow, yet eager to express their feelings for one another. Shelly had noticed that Matthew had a tendency to express himself through actions rather than words. Although this was great for the most part, as she believed actions speak louder than words, sometimes she wished he would open up and tell her how much he liked her, which she hoped he did.

They reached the top of the peak and let their chairs back. They relaxed back in to the seats side by side gazing upwards. They turned to face each other. Matthew lifted his hand to stroke a stray lock of Shelly's hair back off her face. He let out a lustful sigh as he gazed at her and said "Wow, you are so beautiful."

"Thank you," she smiled back at him and shifted forwards. He leant in and pressed his lips against hers, kissing her with a gentle tenderness that sent tingles shivering down her spine. She wanted so badly to feel so much closer to him, and so much more of him.

Before she could seduce him any further with her apparent eagerness,

Matthew paused and pulled away.

"What's wrong?" she asked in a confused and anxious tone. Matthew looked deep into her worried eyes and smiled as he stroked the side of her face.

"Shelly, will you be my girlfriend? I mean, only if you'd like to of course and... well..."

Smiling, Shelly placed a finger to his lips to quiet him and replied, "Hmmmmm, let me think about it." She teased him with a wicked grin spreading across her face.

"Oh...well...in that case..." His heart sank, he felt crushed that she really meant it.

"I'm just joking, silly," she giggled to him at was intended to be an obvious joke, but Matthew looked bewildered. "Of course, I will be your girlfriend Matt, why wouldn't I be?" The question was rhetorical and Shelly leant in and pressed her lips upon his to demonstrate to him how she felt about him.

He placed his arms around her and drew her over on to his side. As they engaged in a passionate embrace, Matthew's hands wandered up and down Shelly's back and over her buttocks. He noticed they were firm and rounded, and he enjoyed pressing his large hands into the small of her back, feeling the contours of her delicious body beneath them. He couldn't resist the urge and slid his hands under her clothes, feeling her soft naked skin mould under the pressure. She slid her hands under his t-shirt and ran them up his spine. He shivered with excitement. She noticed how slender he was and felt the new, unfamiliar sensation of his hot, firm skin beneath her wandering hands. He could feel the tell-tale bulge growing in his pants as he felt his arousal increase and wondered if Shelly could feel it to.

She did and in response reached around and down to his belt, which she unbuckled. Even through his jeans, Shelley could tell he was a big lad, and she was pent up with anticipation. It had been a while and her libido was high. She unbuttoned his jeans and unzipped his fly, pulling it apart to expose his protruding manhood, which fell out and pointed at her. She could see through his underwear that Matthew was very well endowed indeed. She felt her moist excitement trickle down between the top of her thighs, and let him lift off her top and unclasp her bra. She slid his shirt off and noticed he was slim and toned, and she enjoyed drinking in the new sight of his beautiful body. He had a tiny snail trail of dark hair that wandered down to surround his belly button and disappeared beneath him.

Matthew looked upon Shelly for the first time and many sensations overwhelmed him at once. He thought her boobs were sensational; perfectly proportional and well formed, he reached for them and gently squeezed them between his fingers. They spilled over his hands as he caressed them in circles, too big to fit. Matthew felt wonderful as he watched Shelly grow more excited, and felt her pull his underwear down and expose him fully: he reached and undid her jeans as she reached for his massive penis, and felt that she was unable to fit her hand around it.

"Umm, well this is me," he said with a tone of embarrassment and blood rushed to redden his cheeks. He felt nervous; frightened that she would be scared of his size and reject him, like other girls had done before, but not Shelley.

"Mmmmmm, I like you," she smiled at him as she clasped his penis in a firmer grip and rubbed it up and down. Matthew relaxed immediately and smiled back at her, content.

He reached down her sexy underwear and parted her lips, revealing her clitoris. He heard her gasp and felt her grow wet when he touched her. He stroked back up over her swollen clitoris and a pleasurable rush ran up through her and she gasped. His excitement grew as he felt and heard hers. He rubbed up and down on her clitoris, feeling it grow moist and swell. She stroked his shaft in a gentle up and down motion, waves of pleasure rippled through him. He felt her rubbing against him and slid a finger inside her; she let out an audible gasp. He slipped in another one; she was drenched. He moved them around her wet vagina and she groaned as waves of pleasure consumed her.

Matthew maneuvered Shelly so that she was on top of him, facing his penis. He spread her legs and parted her lips, and licked her clitoris. Shelly gasped in response as she felt a tingle of pleasure. Matthew continued to lick at her using a gentle motion, flattening his tongue. This worked perfectly for Shelly who vocalized her enjoyment. Matthew enjoyed hearing her and felt more aroused as he felt her lick up and down his shaft, the vibrations of her moans increasing his stimulation. He took two of his fingers and plunged them inside her and immediately felt her clench over him. Shelly grabbed Matthew's penis in her mouth and sucked on it hard and he let out a groan as he felt himself almost reach climax. He fought to contain it. He plunged his fingers in and out of Shelly and lapped at her sodden genitals. She withdrew from sucking him and howled with pleasure as Matthew brought her to orgasm. She grabbed Matthew's penis in her mouth again and slid it all the way down her throat and cupped his testicles. Matthew couldn't hold back anymore and exploded down her throat. Shelly felt the warm liquid trickle down inside her and sat up to face him when he'd finished.

"Wow, that's some party trick," he beamed at her.

She smiled and crawled back up and kissed him hard. She wriggled down as he sat up and moved his seat and felt herself slide down over on to the tip of his penis. She couldn't help but spread her legs and part her lips to accommodate for him as his massive girth pulled her apart as he entered her. She screamed with pleasure and felt her walls contract over him as she guided him gently inside her. He fought to contain himself and prevented himself from thrusting deep and hard inside her as he felt her consume him. She released a breathless gasp as she felt him slide down inside her. Unable to contain herself, she writhed on top of Matthew, in the car, and sat on the peak of the beautiful spot, under the moonlight, until their furious thrusting brought each other to an intense and ecstatic climax. She felt him throb and the warm liquid filled her spent depths. He felt the sensation wash out of him with ecstatic relief as he came again, inside her.

Matthew turned Shelly on to her side and continued to penetrate her. He felt rejuvenated as she continued to come all over him and felt himself swell inside her again. He moved back and forth, sliding in and out of her as he reached his arms around her in a spooning position. He felt his hands meet her smooth, soft breasts and caressed them. He opened his eyes and drank in the beauty of her amazing body as she writhed back against him in response. He felt the longing pull in his loins as she leant back against him and moaned in his ear. He reached down between her legs and parted her luscious, longing lips to expose her beautiful, swollen, pink labia, which he spread to reveal a swollen protruding clitoris. Matthew felt her excitement grow against him as he pressed his middle finger down on her expectant clitoris and heard her gasp with pleasure in his ear. His own arousal grew and he felt himself grow inside her as his penis felt hot against her convulsing depths. With each stroke, Matthew penetrated deeper in to Shelly's depths; he rubbed his middle finger over her wet, expectant clitoris as he did so, and Shelly began to moan.

She writhed over Matthew, pushing back harder and moving faster as he increased the pace of his finger over her clitoris. She felt the waves of pleasure growing more intense as he brought her closer and closer to climax. Shelly felt the tell-tale signs coursing through her and felt herself clench hard over Matthews massive, hot penis. She thrust her head back against him and cried out as she came, moving hard and faster over Matthew's throbbing penis. Matthew increased his own pace and grunted as he pounded against Shelly in pleasure. They both vocalized their climax as they reached it. An intense throbbing accompanied by a wash of relief washed over him, letting Matthew know that he was there. Shelly felt it flood her depths as they clenched all over his hot throbbing penis. She felt her walls convulse hard over his shaft as he brought her to an intense climax.

A dream is a wish your heart makes, and Shelly's was making hers for Matthew that night, as she dreamt of the moment he would say those three little words.

4 FALLING PART 2
Rear View

Matthew and Shelly had clicked from the moment they met, and they brought out the best in one another. The relationship just worked. They felt comfortable in each others' presence and no silence was awkward. Nothing about either of them was traditional, or conservative, and they often wondered if, perhaps, that's why they worked so well together. Shelly was going away for what felt like a long time, and this would be their last night together.

Sex had always been effortless. They were both easy to please and fancied each other rotten. They were very sexually compatible. Matthew had always found it hard to slow himself down. He got easily excited and carried away. He also found that many women were scared of his penis. Some even, physically, backed off at the sight of it. Shelly, on the other hand, gave him the opposite reaction, when she saw it for the first time. Her face lit up with excitement. He could see how eager she was for him, to feel him inside her for the first time.

"Well, this is me!" He told her, with an apprehensive tone.

"Well, if your ego's as big as your penis, you don't need my input."

"No, but you need mine," he gave her a knowing wink, then, wrapped his arms around her and ravished her, for the first time. She relished every second.

He soon learned her sexual appetite was insatiable. It couldn't be quenched, no matter how often they did it. Sometimes, he felt concerned that this meant he may not be satisfying her, but she assured him she found their sexual experiences very satisfactory.

"I just need more satisfying," she gave him a filthy look. "It's more about quality than quantity, anyway, though I wouldn't mind more quantity," she reiterated, as she leaned in to kiss his neck and ran her naked body down his torso, and guided him, as he slid inside her, yet again. She gasped in his ear and he whispered, "I know there's more to life than sex, but damn, it feels so right with you."

"And you," she confirms, "everything feels so good with you."

Shelly contemplates the fact that she won't have this opportunity, again, for quite some time. So she says to him, "I've wanted to ask you, for a while, but I didn't know how? I feel really nervous saying this, but here it goes...I want to try something."

"OK," an eager smile spreads across his face. He gave her an intrigued look, as she twitched nervously.

"You know how I have a thing for backs," she looks down and smiles, whilst twiddling a stray lock of her hair.

"Yes," he exaggerates his reply.

"Well...You know how you like back rubs..."

"Uh-huh!"

"Well, I'd like to try giving you a special kind of back rub," she looked deep into his eyes and gave him a glimpse of her dirty half smile, as she brought her arms across, in front of her, squeezing her perky breasts together. "She looks so alluring," he thought to himself.

"You know...a hands-free one."

"Ooooooo, yes please," she felt the excitement of his response stiffen beneath her, in eagerness.

"OK, well turn over and I'll lube you up," she leaned forward and gave him a hungry kiss on the lips, as she maneuvered herself, so he could turn round and she could reach for the lube. She squirted a small blob of the cold liquid on her palms and rubbed them together, kissing him with increased intensity; as she did so, he kissed her back with a fierceness that had been absent before, the anticipation only increasing his excitement.

As he turned over, she settled on the small of his back and began stroking herself, down below. She was clean-shaven and, as she parted her lips, he peeked over his shoulder to see her gasp, as she touched her clitoris. He felt his excitement increase. She rubbed her cold palms over his back directly in front of her. Then, she rubbed her warm, wet, pussy into the groove. They groaned in unison, as the pleasure of the pressure and friction combined intensified. He felt her warmth and pressure ease the tense muscles, and his lower spine relaxed. This coupled with the pleasure of hearing her groan, as she writhed on top of him, caused him to groan with enjoyment.

As she looked down, at his long, slender frame, she felt her clitoris swell, as she writhed down hard on it, increasing the pressure and duration with each stroke; she could feel the intensity of the tingling excitement building inside of her. She groaned louder and longer, as she fought to contain it. Warm, wet liquid trickled down the insides of her thighs, as she became increasingly aroused. She'd always had a thing for backs, and getting herself off on his had her feeling so turned on. She was losing herself in the heat of the act. She moaned, uncontrollably, and the pace of her writhing continued to increase.

Her vagina was, now, ready for him. She could feel it open, as the lubricated walls slid and pulled across the soft, smooth skin, just where his butt cheeks started. She felt the slight curve of them make a shallow entry and the pleasurable sensation shot through her like a dose of adrenalin. She screamed her response. She was so close.

He could feel her rampant writhing increase, and he could see it, too. She looked incredible, up there, and having a good time, while she was at it. He could feel the pulses running through her skin, over the top of his butt cheeks. It made them wobble a bit. He could feel they had peeked their way inside her a tad, and he could feel the rest of her moist genitalia, swollen with excitement, gliding over his sopping skin, now soaked, with sexual excitement. He could smell it oozing out of her; it made him feel even more aroused and he shifted, as his penis grew harder and dug into the mattress. He turned his head more and let the sight of her glorious body saturate his, already lustful, eyes. Every curve and crevice was slicked with sweat. He admired the way they wobbled and bounced, in rhythm, to her writhing. She started to touch herself all over, as he noticed her gaze down, at him, her face awash sexual desire.

"You enjoying that?" He asked, with a dirty smirk smeared across his face.

"Mmmm, it's so good!" She exclaimed through orgasmic groans.

"How's the view?"

"Perfect," she glanced down and rubbed across his shoulder blades.

"Ahhhhh, that's good."

"Uhhh..."

"That's it, right there."

He was rather swollen himself. She could feel it, as she ground herself down on him. She felt good knowing that he was enjoying himself as much as she was. Harder and faster she pushed, bringing herself to an explosive orgasm.

"Oh, yeah," she screamed and moaned, as the surge of ecstasy took hold and she lost control. Her writhing became wild, erratic, and frantic. He enjoyed watching her hair fly about her head, into a sexy, tangled, mess, as she finished herself off and slid into the small of his back, and soaked it.

"Tell me how good that feels."

"So fucking gooooooooooood!"

"You're so fucking hot," he told her, as he watched her squirm to a finish. He loved the way she screwed up her face when she came.

He groaned and relaxed into the comfort of the bed with her. As he lay face up, she could gauge just how excited he was. His penis was pointing straight at her, in anticipation. She looked down and smiled, as she gently grasped it in her, still slippery, hands. She caressed it slowly and gently. He tilted his head back and let out a sigh of pleasure. She could feel him; hot and throbbing in her hand, he was more excited than she had realized. She knew she would have to finish him, before she could enjoy fucking him. She slid down and licked his torso, as she did so, careful to avoid his ticklish tummy. She moved her hands down the side of his ribs, round his waist, and down, between his thighs, cupping his testicles. Her tongue followed, and she slowed to a halt, as she reached the sensitive knot at the top of his helmet. Then, she stroked it gently, as she caressed his balls. Her tongue slid up and down his shaft, leaving a trail of saliva from the corner of her mouth.

She admired how perfect his penis was. It was straight, large, and smooth. She could just about wrap her hand around it. She felt he was the perfect size for her. Often, she had felt that she was too big and became too wet, for most guys to really get off having sex with her, but with Matthew, it was different. He was the first man she'd been with where it all just, happened, nice and simple, with no hiccups. Like it was meant to be. They fit each other like lock and key. She couldn't get enough of him, and vice versa. They left each other feeling satisfied, but yearning for more.

He was already near his bursting point, and this just felt like teasing. He wanted her to swallow all of him. So, he told her, "Show us your magic trick, sexy. Make it disappear for me," he smiled down, at her, with a filthy look in his eyes. She stopped and smiled back up, at him. Without a word, she opened her mouth and swallowed him whole. As he slid down her throat, he felt a surge of pleasure course through him and cried out, as it erupted. She felt the warm rush trickle down her throat, as he finished.

She lifted herself up and leaned towards him, straddling him, displaying the front of her body, in all its glory. He caressed each breast simultaneously, as she moved towards him. They felt so soft a malleable, as he cupped and squeezed them from underneath. He moved his fingers up and over them, to her hard, erect, nipples. They appeared to be staring straight at him. He took them in his mouth and began licking and sucking them, as he continued to caress her breasts. She gripped his hair and pulled him towards her, into a fierce kiss. Then, she whispered in his ear, "I want to feel you deep inside me. I want you to make me scream, until you can't hear me anymore. I want…"

"I really want to fuck you so bad," he almost growled at her, through gritted teeth, as he pulled her down, onto him, making her cry out in pleasure.

"Oh yeah, that's it," he grasped her hips and bounced her up and down, on top of him, watching himself slide in and out of her. He enjoyed feeling her become wet with pleasure. She took all of him with ease, sitting down, hard on him, with each bounce, so he could feel the tip of his penis delve into her depths and caress her swelling cervix. He could feel it contract, as he continued to penetrate her. Shelly's screams of pleasure intensified and echoed in his ear, as she leaned over him, her ample breasts swinging in front of him. He couldn't help but grope for them. He wanted something to grab hold of; he was tired of them slipping through his hungry hands.

"I'm coming," she screamed. He grabbed hold of her behind and pulled her onto him, hard, thrusting inside her, as he felt her squirt all over him. She clenched him, as she finished and he groaned. She felt him reach deep inside and her cervix pulsed, as she experienced multiple orgasms and leaked all over him. She could feel him, hot and throbbing inside her, as he came. They came in unison, each feeling the blissful satisfaction of orgasm wash over them.

"Incredible," he sighed.

"Amazing," she confirmed.

They lay there, smiling and gazing at one another. All sense of space and time left them to experience a peaceful aftermath of lust and longing. They held each others' gaze, as they reached out to the other's cheek. They couldn't resist the urge to give it a soft, tender, touch. They cared for each other deeply and both felt fearful the other didn't feel the same way about them. This was not true. Their feelings were shared, equally, and the reassurance of a soft, gentle touch, a tender, prolonged kiss, a random act in the throes of passion, all indicated this. He enjoyed being able to engulf her tiny frame and felt closer every time she asked him for a cuddle. She loved watching him respond to her tender touches and giving him lots of lingering little kisses all over. All the while, he was still inside her. In that moment, their feelings of closeness intensified.

He guided her off him and turned her to face the other way, on all fours. He penetrated her from behind. She gasped with pleasure, as she felt him enter her deep and slow. She rose onto her knees, to meet him, wrapping her arms around his neck, behind her, and pushing down on him. She began to writhe, but he guided her back down, by pressing his hand gently on her back, so her face met the mattress, and in a cheeky tone whispered, "My turn." She obliged, by bending down, on to her elbows, and pushing back onto him, as he drove himself into her, harder and faster, until his balls slapped against her ass. He was now slamming himself inside her, and he was big enough to feel her cervix contracting on him, as she spilt out orgasms, over and over again. She never felt so much of him at once; as she did in this position, it felt almost overwhelming, at times, but in a good way. Her continuous screams of pleasure, coupled with her inability to resist pushing back, indicated to him that she was enjoying it as much as he was. Matthew enjoyed the fact that he never had to worry about her enjoying herself. She was a very lucky woman and had multiples every time. He felt her just keep on cumming, all over him. He kept going and could feel the excitement rising within himself, as he continued to pleasure her, over and over; she was squirting, now, amazingly.

She felt him plunging in and out of her, harder and faster. The waves of pleasure rose higher and higher within her, with each passing stroke, which brought her closer to bliss. She could feel she was squirting, now. The telltale, slippery signs alerted her, as he moved around more and more, inside her. She could still feel him getting even more excited, and he penetrated even deeper, as he did so. She responded, by backing herself into him further and bucking her backside in rhythm with his thrusts.

He loved it when she did that; he could never control himself. It felt so good, and he felt so close to her, as she fought to push him further and further inside her, like they were becoming at one with each other. It was an experience he felt was beyond sexual, and so did she. This was a different kind of connection. He felt himself bend over her, as this feeling of bliss washed over him. He felt his warm skin touch her beautiful, soft curves, as she wriggled with excitement. She rose, to meet him, as he leaned over to give her a passionate, tender kiss. As he did so, the feeling overwhelmed him.

"I'm gonna cum," he groaned, and she responded in kind. Their lips remained locked, as they did so. This was the most intimate moment they had ever shared, and they both felt it. They wanted it to last forever.

"I love you." They both said, at the same time. They fell asleep with him still inside her.

"You know, sometimes this is better than sex," she said to him when they awoke, hours later, their arms entangled in an erotic embrace.

"Is that a good thing?" He asked, bewildered.

"Don't worry silly, there's nothing wrong in that department I assure you, far from it," she giggled.

"Good," he replied and fell back to sleep. She watched his eyelids flicker and his lip twitch, as small snores escaped his cute button nose. She couldn't help but giggle to herself. His lovely long lashes fluttered, like a butterfly in a summer meadow. He looked beautiful, in her eyes. She felt her lust and longing for him return. She couldn't resist the urge any longer. She leaned over and pressed her lips to his. Then, she held him in a long and passionate kiss. He responded, surprised at first, but with equal passion. He placed a hand behind her head and one on the small of her back, then, pulled her towards him.

"You're an amazing and beautiful woman, Shelly," he whispered to her, as he pulled back, to look deep into her eyes. She smiled and kissed him across his cheeks, slow and soft. He felt a stirring in his loins, as his sexual excitement rekindled.

"I'm so glad I told you," she said, pulling her hands through his hair. It was something she did out of habit, but it comforted her, and he enjoyed it.

"Me too," he felt hard, again, and could feel her getting wet, as she felt more turned on. He rolled over and manoeuvred down, under the covers, spreading her legs, as he did so. She felt a warm, wet sensation run across her clitoris, and knew it was his tongue. She felt it, again, and gasped. He knew how much she enjoyed this, and she smiled to herself, as she felt his fingers tracing up and down her inner thighs and into the crevices. She moaned, with pleasure, as the feeling intensified. She felt him give her little licks at irregular intervals; he was such a tease. He kept this up, until she felt she wouldn't be able to bear it any longer. As he felt her begin to wriggle and squirm beneath him, he pressed his tongue down, flat and hard, on her clitoris. He shook his head, vigorously, from side to side, as he buried his face into her. He heard her muffled moan, through a pillow, and knew he was getting the right response. He enjoyed giving, as much as she enjoyed receiving, the pleasure, her pleasure, was all his.

"Mmmmm, you taste delicious," he paused, to tell her.

"Don't stop!" She demanded. He continued to lap up the juices, as they flowed out of her. She felt her sexual arousal increasing and couldn't stop herself from jolting and jerking, as little pulses of pleasure made their way throughout her body. He held her down and worked his tongue over a large area, using a firm, slow pressure. He inserted two fingers inside of her and enjoyed her reaction. She pushed herself up, to meet them. He began to probe inside her. It felt sensitive, as he stimulated her. They fought against one another; as he brought her closer to climax, she rose off the bed, pushing against him, as her heels dug in, her toes curled, and she strained to lift herself against him. He pushed her back down with increased pressure and the pleasurable sensations she was experiencing heightened.

"Fuck yeah," she cried out, as he almost got her there. She began to move back and forward, against his movement, rubbing herself on him as much as he rubbed his tongue against her. She could feel it continuing to build up, until it washed over her, and she felt herself cumming in short, sharp bursts of relief. He'd gently brought her to an intense orgasm.

"I'm cumming," she jerked on his tongue and clenched on his fingers. He looked up and noticed her rosy glow, and peaceful expression. She always got it, just after an orgasm. He admired the rise and fall of the peaks and troughs of her beautiful feminine form, as she closed her eyes and smiled. He pulled himself up and lay behind her. She knew he was watching her, as she felt his gentle touch stroke up and down her side.

She nestled into him, so they were spooning, and gripped his fully erect penis between her thighs. Then, she started sliding over it. It felt so good he couldn't help but let out a gasp of pleasure. He reached over her shoulder and placed his hand between her saturated lips. He felt her swollen and expectant clitoris and began to stroke her. She moved with him, as he brought her many pleasurable orgasms. Matthew felt the bed sheets soaking, beside him, and he couldn't resist any longer. As she pulled away, he slipped his penis up, inside her. She gasped and pushed herself back, onto him, and began to thrust on him. As she felt increasingly stimulated, she began to arch her back and moan. He pulled her onto him, harder, as she continued to cry out in pleasure.

"Fuck me back!" She demanded. He obliged. Each thrust caused her to scream louder and her pitch became higher.

"Oh yeah, yeah! Yes!" She exclaimed as she experienced a particularly intense orgasm. He pushed her forward. The angle had an immediate effect on them both.

"Christ yes!" He exclaimed, as he felt more of her and delved deeper inside.

"Oooooooooooooo...Mmmmmmmmmmmm m...YES!" She responded, as she felt him penetrate new depths.

"I'm gonna cum," he warned her. She responded by pressing herself back against him, tilting her head back, and reaching to kiss him, while moving herself up and down, on his massive, throbbing penis, harder and faster. She began squirting all over it, as the feeling of ecstasy consumed them both and she felt his warm, wet release fill her, as he felt it empty out of him. As the orgasmic feelings dissipated, the connection returned. She felt so good with him, so close in that moment, that she didn't want it to end. He felt the same, as he gave a blissful sigh and wrapped his arms around her. He nestled his face into her neck, kissing it, over and over. She felt little tingles pulsate through her, in response to his affections. They reassured her, this was so much more.

"Oh, my! Is that the time!" She exclaimed, as she jumped up, out of bed, and bent over to grab her clothes. He knew he wouldn't see her for what felt like ages. He knew he wouldn't be able to do this with her for weeks. He watched his semen seep out of her, still swollen, lips. As she bent over, he could still see inside her. He could still see that she was aroused and wanting. She still wanted him inside of her.

He sprang out of bed and took her by surprise, from behind. She gasped, in a confused daze of shock and pleasure. She placed her hands on the floor, in front of her, to steady herself, as he banged against her beautiful bottom one last time. He made sure he enjoyed and admired every tiny part of it. He stroked, grabbed, caressed, and slapped it with one hand, while he reached round to pleasure her, from the front, with the other. This was the deepest and most intense angle he could enter her and he plunged in and out of her, now gapping, vagina, wet and wide, from hours of constant abusive pleasure with him.

She felt him protrude deep within her, and she found herself gasping in shrill excited breaths, as it stimulated new and intense feelings inside her. They washed through her body, as he continued to pound her from behind, standing over her. She could feel him getting more excited. The feelings of pleasure intensified, as she felt herself reaching, yet, another climax. Her walls clenched his ever-expanding penis. It began to throb, as they thrust against one another, harder and faster. With a final release, he pulled her onto him, so he was deep inside her, as he groaned to a finish. She squirted on him, again, and he watched it splash, as it hit the floor. She gave one final push back and writhed on his, now, spent penis, as she finished herself with moans of pleasure. They knew this was it. She had to go, now.

5 FALLING PART 3
Teasing

It had felt like an eternity to them both, but Shelly finally arrived back from her trip to the other side of the world, and Matthew picked her up from the airport. She ran to him and they engaged in a passionate embrace. They kissed each other, furiously. Matthew felt his excitement begin to rise, while Shelly felt herself melt in his familiar arms.

"I've missed you so much," he whispered in her ear.

"I've missed you, too," she kissed him full and hard, on the lips, cupping his face in her hands. "So, so much," she smiled up, at him.

They decided to stop for the night, in a beautiful little boutique hotel, just outside of the city. It was a rural location set deep in the countryside.

Matthew led Shelly up the grand elaborate staircase and turned the key in the lock of door nineteen, their home for the night. It was spacious with high ceilings. A tall, grand fireplace stood against the main wall, and elaborate decor covered its walls and ceilings, throughout. An iron cast, king-sized, four-poster bed, adorned with decorative features, was placed in the centre. Its rich, velvety, crimson linen welcomed them over to it.

Matthew led Shelly to the bed and she sat down, on its edge. He sat beside her and stroked her cheek upward, then delved his fingers into her hair. He pulled her toward him, into a fierce embrace and a hard, passionate kiss. Shelly responded and wrapped her arms around him, pulling at his t-shirt.

"God, I love you!" he told her, as he stared deep into her eyes.

"I love you so much," she shook her head and stroked his face, as she replied.

She started to kiss him, again, with a gentle tenderness that sent tingles down both of their spines. He undid the buttons on her blouse, with practiced efficiency, and gently slipped it off her shoulders. As he kissed her, he reached behind her and unclasped her bra, than slid it off. He reached for her full, succulent breasts. He grasped them in his hands and caressed them in a circular motion, the memories flooding back to him. He remembers her taste, smell, and texture, and how good they all are. Shelly's breathing became more erratic. She felt waves of pleasure flow through her. He leaned down and slowly circled his tongue around her areola, working his way to her nipple. Shelly let out an audible sigh, as her arousal reached its center. He repeated the same motion, on the other side. She felt the pleasurable sensations coursing through her nipples and throughout her body. Her genitals grew warm and wet, as she imagined what was about to transpire.

Shelly pulled his t-shirt over his head; she was feeling really turned on, now. He undid the zipper on her skirt and she stood up, as he pulled it down. As it slid around her ankles, he gasped, as he realized she wasn't wearing any panties. He wore a filthy smile on his face, as he looked up, at her, and said, "Tut, tut. Naughty girl." He pretended to tell her off.

"You love it really," she gave him a filthy smirk.

"True, true." He leaned forward and cheekily slipped his tongue between her lips. She gasped.

"Hey! Not so fast!" She scolded him and stepped away. He felt the response in his loins and knew he was hard. As he enjoyed looking upon her beautiful feminine form, he felt his arousal increase and resisted the urge to touch himself. He wanted this to last.

She stood naked, before him. He watched, as she lifted her fingers to her mouth and licked them. She inserted them inside her mouth and began to suck on them, mock moaning a pleasurable response. She trailed the back of her hand, slowly and sensually down, over her body, starting at her neck and finishing down, over her collarbone. She continued over her breast and down, past her navel. She released a long breath, as she reached down and parted her lips. Then, she began to stroke herself. Matthew's eyes lit up, as he watched her. She felt herself become wet, as she stimulated herself to a blissful arousal. He went to reach for her.

"No," she told him. "You can watch, I'm going to tease you now," she flashed him a wicked smile.

As she continued to rub herself, she felt more and more aroused. She closed her eyes, tilting her head back, releasing quiet moans of pleasure. As she felt herself relax, she moved toward the bed, there lay her favourite toy. It was large, but not as big as Matthew. She stared at his swollen and expectant penis, taking in how it looked. The memories began flooding back to her. She felt herself grow warmer, as she watched it lean toward her in anticipation. She remembered how it felt when he was inside her. She wanted to feel him inside her so much, but she restrained herself. She was going to make sure that she gave him the best buildup, after his long, long wait, while she had her fun.

The toy was long and girth-like. A bright, glittery magenta, it was shaped like, but did not resemble in appearance, a penis, of any fashion. It had a much smaller, banana-shaped protrusion, from its base, alongside the main shaft, which angled toward it. It was designed for double stimulation.

She took it in one hand, as she continued pleasuring herself with the other. She crawled, on her knees, onto the bed, moaning loudly. She handed her toy to him and said, "I want you to fuck me with this, as hard and as fast as you can. You can watch me scream with excitement, while you wait for yours."

"With pleasure," he leaned over and whispered in her ear, inserting her toy inside her, as he did so. She was so dripping wet; it slid in with little resistance. She released a sharp breath, as it penetrated her and arched her back, into him, to engulf it. He began to thrust it in and out of her. She released groans of enjoyment, as he did so. He leaned back and she rose, to meet it with his movement.

She could feel the toy's dual stimulator stroke her clitoris in rhythm with the thrusts, as he plunged it in and out of her engorged vagina, drenched with sexual excitement. She lie, face down, rear up, on the bed, as he continued to thrust the plastic pleasure in and out of her, harder and faster, as she grew closer and closer to climax. He flicked the switch and the intensity of her arousal instantly amplified, as the telltale buzz caused the toy to stimulate new pleasures deep within, in and out of her. She pushed back, as he drove it in and out of her, over and over, harder and faster. The vibrations tickled her cervix, which contracted frantically, as her sodden vagina clenched over the mobile shaft. As he brought her to an intense climax, she threw her head back and let out a scream of ecstasy. He slowed the movement, as she finished, her waves of orgasmic pleasure rippling over it, as he withdrew it from her.

She took it from him and placed it between his legs. She stood at the end of the bed and sat back, onto it, as he reached up and let out a gasp in his ear. She tilted her head to kiss him, as she began to bounce up and down on the toy clenched between his thighs. As she did so, it stimulated her from in front and she felt the intense sexual stirrings heighten, as she brought herself to another climax.

Shelly reached for Matthew's desperate erection, soothing some of its sexual agony, as she grasped it in her hand and caressed it. He released a deep groan of satisfied relief, as he felt her warm hands stimulate him, to near climax, there and then. He watched, over her shoulder, and had his arms wrapped in front of them. Her breasts were cupped in his hands and he tweaked her nipples with his fingers. Her boobs jiggled between them, as she moved up and down on her toy, in front of him. The sight of seeing her stimulate herself to such ecstasy, as she caressed him, knowing that, at some point soon, he was going to be able to do that to her himself and feel the warm release, as she climaxed on him and screamed her delight at him, for giving it to her. The thoughts were overwhelming and he almost felt them get the better of him. He gently guided her hand away as he felt her pace increase with the excitement and almost finish him before he was ready.

She bounced up and down, deeper between his thighs, feeling all of the toy reach deep inside her and all of her lips and swollen clitoris being stimulated in unison. She felt the growing intensity of both sensations, together, well and rise up, within her. As she reached her peak, the excitement overwhelmed her and she cried out, louder than she ever had before. As she climaxed, she squirted all over them both, drenching everything around her. She sank herself hard, down, onto the toy between his thighs and leaned back and then bucked herself over it. She felt it stimulate her cervix and she wailed with a new release of orgasmic pleasure, as she experienced all three stimuli, at the same time. She collapsed back, into him, as she finished.

As she lay on her back, on the bed, exhausted, he leaned over her and whispered in her ear, "I think I've waited long enough, now."

He straddled her, parting her legs, so she lay with them spread on either side of him. He tilted her pelvis toward him and slid inside her. She felt soaked down there, and so was he. They were both incredibly slippery. She wrapped her legs around him and slid herself over him, in rhythm to his quick, sharp thrusts. He grunted, as he slid himself in and out of her. She felt the stirrings of more orgasms, as she slid herself over his slippery skin. He moved harder and faster, in and out of her. She moaned, as he did so. As he felt himself unable to hold onto his load any longer, he grabbed her legs and pinned them behind her, as he drove himself down, into her, as he felt the warm rush explode out of him and into her. He felt her respond as he throbbed, and she contracted over him, in unison, shrinking over his expanding penis. She felt him bring her to another intense orgasm, as he dug down, into her depths, and she felt the pressure from his tip on her cervix, causing all of her to contract hard, over his throbbing penis. She experienced a clitoral orgasm, as she slid over him, again, and finished with a squirt of warm sexual juices, drenching their already soaked and slippery bodies.

They awoke, hours later, their legs entwined and still wet from their previous shenanigans. They gazed at each other, smiling, feeling the warmth of the closeness radiate between them. Matthew began stroking Shelly's arm. It felt so smooth beneath his rough palm. He felt her start stroking up his back. It sent tingling sensations radiating down his spine. He slipped his hand under her arm and ran it down her back. He felt the curve of her arch, where her back met her buttocks, and he spread his palm over her firm, pert cheek and grasped it. They were kissing with intent. A fierce lust for one another now passed between them. They began running their hands up and down, all over each others' bodies, moving round to the front, as they ran their hands up and down, over one another. Matthew placed his hands over Shelly's breasts, cupping them as best he could. She had full, ample breasts that over spilled his hands. He moved his face toward them and shook it between them. Shelly giggled at him.

"You don't know how much I've wanted to do that for so long!" He smiled up at her. She laughed long and loud.

"You can do that as much as you like," she told him.

"Don't worry, I will," he confirmed and dived back in.

He ran his hands down her sides and followed her body shape round and down between her thighs. He felt her relax, as he parted them slightly. As he leaned up to kiss her, he parted her lips and slid a finger between them. She gasped the instant he made contact with her moist clitoris and felt her gush a new release of wetness on to his hand.

"It's been a while," she smiled at him.

"Indeed, it has," he replied.

Matthew sprang up and maneuverd Shelly, so she lay with her legs dangling over the edge of the bed. He spread them wide open and knelt before her. Shelly felt the tingling sensation course through her ripe and ready body, as he made contact with her swollen genitalia. She gasped and moaned, as he ran his tongue up and down, at a slow pace, over her entire area.

Shelly felt herself relaxing on him as he probed into her. She felt him run his tongue around, inside her. She felt the pleasure well up, from within her, and cried out her response. He ran his tongue back up and over her clitoris, and flicked it at a fast pace, while inserting two of his fingers in and out of her. He felt her contract over them, as he stimulated her and heard her cry out.

She felt herself twitch and jerk, as pulses of pleasure shot through her, while he licked and flicked his tongue over her, faster and faster. Just as she felt she was about to explode in an orgasmic response, he suddenly slowed and flattened his tongue over her. He rubbed it up and down. She felt it sliding against her. New, calmer sensations began welling from her clitoris. At the same time, he moved his fingers in and out of her, harder and faster, and she felt herself clenching over him, as he brought her to a penetrative climax, over and over. As the sensations increased, she felt herself reach orgasms on both levels. Then, she drenched his hand and face. He lapped it up and she rose to meet another orgasm, as he took in the taste of her sweet ecstasy. After he cleared enough, so as not to leave her dripping too much, he stood and lifted her legs. He spread them, either side of him, and she wrapped them around his waist, pulling him toward her. He rammed himself inside her and she screamed, as she came through penetration alone. He felt her clench onto him, and he felt the intensity of the stimulation within him increasing. He slowly thrust himself in and out of her, rubbing his thumb over the tip of her clitoris, as he did so. He felt her writhing against him, and he pulled himself in and out of her, entering her over and over again, watching himself be engorged by her wet and hungry swollen lips. He felt them grasping at him, over and over, fighting to keep him inside. Eventually, he succumbed and leaned over her. He groaned, as he let himself probe deeper and deeper inside her, until he reached the bottom of her depths. He felt them respond, as his tip rubbed against it. He wanted to bring her to a slow and sensual orgasm, but he couldn't resist the urge, as he felt her writhing beneath him, moaning with pleasure. He paused for a moment. Then, she increased her pace against him and screamed. "Don't stop! Fuck me harder! I've wanted to feel you inside me for so long."

He responded and enjoyed watching himself sliding in and out of her, over and over. She noticed what he was doing. He was delighted to watch her prop herself up and do the same. She felt hotter, with both excitement and mild embarrassment, as she watched Matthew's penis enter in and out of her, over and over. She was amazed to watch herself make him disappear and enjoyed the pleasure she felt when he did so. They felt themselves growing closer to climax and increased their pace against one another. As Matthew felt himself almost come, he withdrew and flipped Shelly over, so she lay flat on her stomach. He leaned over her and entered from behind. She screamed as he brought her to a penetrative orgasm. She pushed her buttocks up, to meet him, as he drove down into her. She felt new sensations engulf her, as he slid inside her, deep and hard. He thrust himself, furiously, in and out of her. He cried out into the mattress, as he felt the sensation rise and overwhelm him. It exploded out of him, in a warm rush, into her. He felt her writhe and jolt against him, as she finished with him. Shelly felt herself cum, as the warm rush filled her from within. She screamed with pleasure, as she slid her contracting cervix over Matthew's spent penis.

Shelly was feeling hornier and sexier than ever, and she wanted more. She was not satisfied, as she felt Matthew start to slump over her. So, she turned herself around, with him still inside her, onto all fours, and started pushing back against him. To his surprise, Matthew felt himself responding almost immediately, gazing down, at the love of his life's beautiful, ripe buttocks, certainly helped, as he felt the stirrings of sexual arousal rise from within. He felt himself reach down and caress her soft skin with his hands. He felt stimulated, but not fully. He noticed that he was not full and hard, inside Shelly, and he barely touched her sides, as she moved herself around, on him. She was wet and gapping; he could see right inside of her, as she lay open, over him. Seeing the space still to be filled gave Matthew an idea.

He reached for the still wet and slippery toy, and gazed over it, as Shelly continued to push back, onto his still semi-stimulated penis. He reached under her and wiped the toy over Shelly's drenched genitals. He felt and heard her response, as she moaned louder and pushed back harder onto him. As she pulled forward, he inserted the sodden toy inside her, along with his half-soft penis. It filled Shelly, immediately. She screamed and slammed herself down onto him and the toy. Matthew felt himself expanding with excitement at her response. She cried out, longer and louder, as she felt it. Having both inside her, at once, felt huge. She could feel herself stretching and the pleasurable shock waves it sent coursing through her, as Matthew expanded with the toy still inside her. She felt them both start to move, and the increased friction, causing her sexual excitement to rise, with every stroke. She couldn't help but cry out and move with them. Matthew turned the toy and made contact with Shelly's clitoris and then turned it on. Shelly immediately came and squirted all over him. She launched herself up and down, on Matthew and the toy, harder and faster than he'd ever seen her go before. She felt the distinct shapes of them, as she contracted over them, over and over, as she climaxed, continually, as she was simultaneously stimulated by Matthew and the vibrating toy.

Matthew fought to control himself, as he made Shelly feel more satisfied than ever before. He guided her over, so she had her buttocks pointing up toward him. He enjoyed watching himself and the toy plunging in and out of her squirting vagina, over and over. It felt pretty tight on him now, and he could feel his excitement swelling up, inside his penis. He enjoyed thrusting the toy in and out of her, harder and faster. He felt it stimulate him, as it rubbed against his shaft, the small vibrations stimulating him to new heights. He began to moan, as he felt himself drawing closer to orgasm. He could feel Shelly reaching hers, too. She felt tighter and tighter, over him, as he felt waves of contractions from her glide over his throbbing penis.

Shelly felt the inevitable release, as a mighty orgasm consumed her and sent her thrusting herself furiously upward to engulf Matthew and the toy as much as she could. He drove himself and the toy down into her, making her scream with orgasmic delight, as he felt the pleasure well up and out of him. Shelly's orgasm was hard and lasted for a long time. Matthew was spent, before she had finished contracting over him and the still vibrating toy. She had engulfed them both, and even some of Matthew's hand, he'd never seen her so hot and horny before, and never felt so aroused and satisfied himself.

"That was amazing!" he said.

"Amazing," she confirmed, with a smile.

6 THE PRINCE

They had been running for what felt like hours, and at their pace, hundreds of miles were behind them. As they breached the forest edge, they slowed. When they were deep inside and covered by the canopy, they stopped in a small clearing. Constellina had to stop herself short; otherwise, she would have tripped over the figure lying sprawled out, in front of her.

It was post-battle, and her first reaction was to draw her sword, but she soon realized that what she had stumbled across was an unconscious, human male. Her keen, almond-shaped, sky blue eyes clocked the symbol he adorned round his powerful neck.

"Aurora, over here," she called, for her

lover's attention. Aurora shot through the vegetation, swifter than the human eye could follow, and was by her partner's side, in a flash, gazing down, at her discovery.

"It's the Prince," she pointed to the medallion, engraved with the royal symbol.

"He's very handsome, for a human," they both thought, as they gazed upon the helpless figure. He didn't stir, at all, not even a slight snort of a nostril. He appeared dead, but for the rise and fall of his chest, and the sound of his breathing, only apparent to their elfin senses.

They gazed upon each others' beautiful faces. Each angle was so precise and perfect; it highlighted the extent of their differences to the Prince's very attractive, but ordinary, features. Certain aspects of him appeared quite extraordinary. What surprised the elfin maids most about him was his height, still apparent in his horizontal state. He must have been at least six and a half foot, if not more. The same height as Constellina, who, for an elf, was only average height for a female. Elves stood, on average, over a foot taller than most humans. It was very rare for Constellina to come across a human male who was on her eye level.

Aurora, on the other hand, was very petite for an elf woman, standing at just under six foot. This, coupled with her unusually voluptuous and curvy frame, meant she was sometimes mistaken for being a very tall and beautiful human woman, but a closer look would reveal otherwise. She was aesthetically far more appealing than any human could ever hope to be, as was her lover.

They feel the adrenaline-like effects, caused by the battle, still coursing through their veins, leaving the lovers wanting a release. As they gaze upon his half-naked form, they begin to feel the stirrings of sexual arousal. Although their hearts belong to each other, they still appreciate the attraction of the masculine form, and they have another motivation.

"I am still without child," Aurora sighs in desperation.

"As am I," Constellina reflects her confirmation.

They had been trying to fulfil their greatest desire for some time, but without success, or support. Shunned by their race for their sinful relationship and forced to exist with only each other for company, they became even more desperate to fulfil their greatest wish.

Together, they absorb the strength that seems to radiate from the man's broad, athletic body. His shoulders are broad and well set, laced with sinewy muscle. His abs are apparent and protrude through his skin, in a familiar pattern. They trace it with their eyes and lick their lips in anticipation. As their gaze travels down, to his member, a hot flush rises to their cheeks. They do not want to hold back any longer, they are too impatient to wait for him to awaken.

The elves bend down and lean over him. They lock lips and embrace over him. Then, they reach down each other's tunic simultaneously. They gasp, as their fingertips reach their targets. Having spent the last few weeks engaged in near-constant battle, the lovers had little time to indulge in the wonders of each other's sexual desires. Aurora's excitement heightened. In the heat of the moment, she made a feisty move and gives the Prince a passionate kiss on the lips. They cannot fail to notice his loin cloth rise before them. He awakens and takes the kissing maiden by the back of her head, sits up, and responds to her. He reaches under her tunic to stroke her angular, perky breast, with one hand. Her nipple is cold as ice and hard as stone. She whimpers, as he caresses it. He feels the other elfin maiden pull his loin cloth aside and reach for his manhood. He has yet to open his eyes, but he can feel nothing but glorious beauty and their magnificent scent surround him. He hungers for more and feels his member throbs as it is grasped firmly by the expectant elfin maiden.

Constellina gasps, in shock at its size. It would be more than enough to please them both. As he continues his embrace with her elfin lover, she straddles him and he enters her elfin depths. He feels surprised, as she engulfs all of him and sits down hard, as she writhes upon him. He hasn't had a woman for so, so, long, and he releases his pent-up frustrations within her, immediately. His initial reaction is to feel guilty, as he hasn't had a chance to please her yet. But, he hears her scream with ecstasy and feels her mess all over his still throbbing manhood. He relaxes as he realizes she was enjoying it.

He lays back and the other elf, having been so turned on to see her lover respond to him, straddles his face and begins to rip her clothes off, as they kiss each other with intent. He feels her moist womanhood become more excited as she begins to drip all over him. He strokes her buttocks, from behind, and grasps them, as he feels more turned on. He enjoys how good it feels to have such perfect feminine form in his grasp. Constellina is still astride him, and he is still inside her. He feels himself growing within her, and she feels it, too; she writhes around on him in response, her womanhood, now smaller and less slippery than before. He feels her begin to contract and squeeze his manhood into hot and throbbing excitement. He pulls the other elf maid down, onto him, and plunges his tongue deep inside her. She feels him enter her and gasps an aroused response. He gropes her firm and ample buttocks as he guides her over his face, licking deep into every crevice he meets. Her excitement heightens, and she increases her pace over his face, while kissing and caressing her now naked lover, who is still astride the prince's penis and riding him hard.

The lovers feel so stimulated, seeing each other so sexually aroused. They rub their slippery bodies all over each other, breast upon perfect, pert breast, making contact over and over. He feels hips glide over him, as their excitement continues to increase. He plunges two of his long, large fingers into the elf maid above him and is surprised to find they soon disappear. He continues to plunge into her, until his fingers won't reach any further and is pleased to hear her moan with pleasure. He continues to lick her angular clitoris and feels the fluid fall from her, as she reaches her climax, on his face. This other elf maid reaches her climax with her lover, and, as she finishes, her pace increases and brings him to finish. He groans, as he feels the release rush out of him. They sigh and pause, as they acknowledge they've climaxed in unison.

Eager, as he is, the Prince is spent, for now, but the elves are just getting started. They stand over him in a naked embrace. As he admires their bodies, a feeling of lust becomes him. One is so petite and feminine, for an elf, he'd never seen one adorned with such curvature before. Her waist nipped into a tiny circumference, yet her hips broadened and she was blessed with big, perky, breasts. He felt aroused, as he watched them jiggle and bounce with every little movement she made. The other elf was much taller, at his eye level, and he was very tall for a human. She had a slimmer, more athletic build, also beautifully toned, which was only enhanced by the reflection of her snow-white skin. Her breasts were small and angular in comparison, but still very pleasing to the eye, and they would still fill most of his hand, if he cupped them, he was not displeased with what he saw by far. They both had beautiful, long lean legs and shapely bottoms, one rounder and more shapely, the other very toned and athletic, but both still a beautiful sight by anyone's standards.

They reached down and touched each other's womanhood. Then, there was a brief pause from their kissing, to gasp and smile at one another, as they did. The smaller, red-haired elf knelt before her lover, placed her palms between her lover's thighs, and parted her lips. The tall, fair elf placed her hands upon her lover's head and smiled down, at her. The red-haired elf licked slowly up, between her parted lips and stared up, at her lover, who gasped. The Prince felt a stirring in his loins, as he watched. It soon pulled down, into his penis, and when he looked down, at himself, he was hard, again. This was, no doubt, the most spectacular sexual display he had ever witnessed, let alone been a part of. As he watched the elfin maid please her lover, as she knelt over him, he couldn't help himself.

He shifted his position, so that he was facing away from the elves and slid underneath the red-headed elf, as she knelt before her lover, still pleasing her with every flick of her tongue. They were so absorbed in one another that they didn't notice, and the red-haired elf cried out, as he made contact with his tongue. She stumbled forward, into her lover, so that her tongue delved into her depths. The blonde elf moaned a pleasurable response. He grabbed hold of her buttocks and guided her down, onto his face, again. As he brought her to ecstasy, before she did her lover, he became so aroused that he knelt up, behind her, and penetrated her. She pushed back, onto his massive member and grabbed her lover round the waist, pulling her womanhood onto her face. She took three fingers and slid them inside her lover's wet vagina, as she wriggled her tongue hard, over her clitoris, which caused her to cry out, as she came hard. The sight and sound of the two climaxing elfin women was enough to finish him, for a third time. He stayed inside the red haired elf and asked her to lie back on top of him, so that he may stroke and caress her beautiful body to a slow and sensual orgasm, while he remained inside her. As he descended, with her still upon him, she turned and kissed him, a lustful look in her eyes. They had chosen well. This man was a fine specimen, for any race. She hoped his seed would be planted in at least one of their barren bodies. For this reason, she was even keener to allow him to stay inside her.

He enjoyed feeling the form of her body merge into his. He caressed her breasts and reached down, to stimulate her protruding womanhood. Her lover knelt before them and began to pleasure them both, sliding her tongue up, over his testicles and around her lover's moist, wet genitals. The Prince and the elf maid groaned with enjoyment, as the blonde elf knelt before them. He felt himself rise inside her, again. Her response was immediate, as she writhed on top of him and came over and over. He started thrusting himself into her, as he slowed and cupped her breasts together and leaned over her shoulder. He enjoyed watching them wobble. The blonde elf was still on her knees, stimulating them.

Before he finished, again, the red-haired elf got up. She was so fast he had to double take. Her lover began to follow. She stuck her buttocks high into the air, as she stood bent over with straight legs, her hands on the floor, her womanhood gapped, vacant, and expectant. He couldn't resist, as he watched his juices, from their earlier shenanigans, drip out of her. He jumped up and penetrated her hard, slamming all of himself deep into her. He groaned as he did so. He pressed his hand down, on her back, to steady her, and pounded into her from behind. She gasped in surprise, he felt huge inside her, filling all the space she had. He was long enough to find the bottom of her, and he stimulated her entire being into writhing ecstasy, as she bucked her backside and pushed it back into him, wanting him to go deeper. She wanted his seed to fill her, as deep as possible, to try and make sure he would give them the child they so desperately wanted. As he finished, she made sure she sat back hard on his penis and tilted her buttocks skyward to avoid spilling his seed, as he withdrew.

Her lover realized what she was doing and felt awash with guilt, thinking, of how much of his precious seed spilled and wasted so far. She wasted no time. She advanced over, to the man, and demanded he fuck her as hard and fast as possible, until he spilled his seed inside her and filled her to the brim. Being a gentleman, the Prince asked the lady how best he could please her. She asked him to penetrate her with her legs behind her head, as deep as possible. She knelt and drew him down, on top of her, as she told him. He stiffened, as she grasped his manhood in her hand. She guided him inside her and pushed up, onto him, pulling him deep inside her. While her lover remained in position and watched, she continued to let his seed seep into her. She decided to enjoy watching him implant himself into her lover, as much as possible, and brought herself to climax over and over again, as she watched.

He lifted himself up, on to his strong, muscular arms and thrust in and out of the elfin maid. Now helpless, with orgasmic ecstasy, she screamed over and over; while each thrust penetrated her deeper than the last, he warned her he was nearly spent, lifted her legs back, and tilted her hips further, as he drove himself into her one last time. The final throb took the remaining seed from inside him and dispersed into her depths. He withdrew and collapsed with exhaustion. The red-haired elf remained with her womanhood pointing skyward, rocking back and forth, to disperse his seed. Once they were done, the elfin maids left in the blink of an eye. The sleeping Prince was, now, oblivious to his surroundings.

7 THE PRINCE PART 2
The Werewolf

The Prince travelled with elfin maids at a sedate pace, through the forest, unaware just how much he slowed their progress, but they did not care. They were delighted to have him accompanying them, pleasuring them both, and filling them with his seed, at will. The Prince was always willing to please them. As they rest, one night, following a particularly intense session, the Prince sat up and exclaimed, "Oh no! How many nights have passed, since you found me? When will the moon next be full?" The Prince sounded desperate, frightened.

"A full lunar cycle has transpired, since we first found you, your Majesty," Constellina informed him. Panic filled the Prince's eyes, as she told him.

"So tonight, the moon is full, tonight?"

"Yes," she responded.

"Run! Run! You must run!" He insisted. His jerking became more frantic, and he stooped over, clutching the sides of his head, gripping his hair, and tearing it out, as he did so. Constellina and Aurora watched, in horror, as the Prince began to grow before them, and what they witnessed shocked them to the core.

The moon shone full and bright above them; it peeked its way through the clearing, in the canopy, and bathed him in moonlight. As he transformed, it dawned upon the elves what he was. His nose and jaw lengthened, into an ugly snout, which became a muzzle. His lips pinned back, to reveal a set of protruding canine teeth. His eyes filled black and his ears rose, to the top of his head and out pointed, skyward. As his forelimbs lengthened, his hands and feet curled, into paws. As his nails thickened, to claws, his torso stopped over, and he placed all four limbs on the ground, threw his head back, and let out a blood-curdling howl.

The elves moved swift, through the forest, but the Prince was faster. Constellina, being the more athletic of the two, pulled away, at a blinding pace, and left Aurora to eat her dust. It was a matter of minutes, before she heard the wolf's low rumbles behind her. She made the mistake of looking back, and before she knew it, he was upon her.

Aurora was cornered, there was nowhere to run. The werewolf could out sprint her, in any direction, fast as she was. This was a creature, even more supernatural than she. His scent lingered in her nostrils. The stench was enough to make her wretch. It was all over her. The Prince approached her. She expected it to be quick and viscous, but she heard him pause. As the pause seemed to last for hours, she glanced at him, through her hair, and what she saw disturbed her, more than when she thought he was about to kill her. He stood there, on his hind legs, in front of her, head tilted to the side, coal black eyes staring straight at her. A low, unfamiliar rumble escaped his lips, but he wasn't bearing his teeth. Something caught her eye, as she stared. It was a dark red, long and cylindrical, in shape, and grew slightly bulbous at the end. It was longer than her hands and too thick to grasp, and pulsated wildly. As she realized what it was, the sight terrified her. He was intending to mate with her! "No!" She thought. "No, the horror! What if I conceive? No, abomination!" The thought left her feeling petrified. "I'm, I'm... It's the right time in my cycle." Her heart sank, as she realized the wolf had, now, approached her, on all fours.

As the wolf's nose prodded her mound, protruding through her tunic, she wept. Cries of desperation and hopelessness escaped her. She knew, if she didn't comply, it would be her end. This was her only hope of survival. As the Prince watched her tears fall, this melts his, still human, heart and he returns to his human form and tells Aurora, "I want you as a man."

As he runs the back of his hand down her body, starting at her cheek and finishing between her legs. Aurora spreads them, in response, and tilts her head back, to kiss the hungry Prince. His hand slips beneath a gap, in her tunic, and he pulls it aside to expose her. He feels her juices leak on his fingers, as he does so. Her kisses are hungry, as she tastes his mouth with her tongue. She raises her leg over his hip, as she grasps his, now firm, manhood and draws him towards her. As he flicks her clitoris with his fingers, he brings her to a screaming orgasm. Then, she takes his expectant penis and guides it inside her. He feels his excitement rise and pushes himself into her, as he makes contact with her wet, elfin womanhood. She rises, to meet him, and cries out, as he does. The Prince plunges himself in and out of her, over and over, harder and faster, as he brings himself closer to climax. Aurora reached down and continued to stimulate her clitoris, as the Prince brought her to a penetrative orgasm, over and over again. She felt herself cum, as she felt him throb against her walls and release his warm, wet seed, inside her. He kisses her, as he withdraws.

"I want nothing, but to please you, Aurora. You are more beautiful to me than a moonless night."

He kneels before her, stripping her down and exposing her flesh, taking in the stunning silhouettes created by her glorious feminine form, in the colours of the night. He drank her beauty, as he stared up and saw her leaning back, against the tree. He reaches forward and licks up her thigh, towards her soft centre. The excitement overwhelms him, as he touches the tip of her, still moist and swollen, clitoris. An agonizing cry escapes him, as he transforms back, into a werewolf, pinning Aurora, with her back against the tree, and takes her for his own.

She feels his tongues lengthen and flatten, making its way inside her; his muzzle pushes upwards, against her clitoris, and she feels powerful pleasurable sensations rush upwards, as the Prince moves his, now cold, wet nose against her.

As she becomes more aroused, she lets out screams of sexual excitement, tainted with fear. The Prince keeps moving against her and brings her to orgasm, as he continues his transformation. As she finishes, she looks down, into his coal black eyes.

Aurora turns, to face the tree. The wolf pushes its muzzle between her legs and licks between her legs. The sensation was wet and sloppy, as its huge canine tongue licked firm, over her. She spread her legs, as she felt herself relax, down, onto him. She couldn't help but let out a gasp, as it caused familiar sensations to course through her body. She stood before him, naked, and was helpless, as he ravaged her to a decadent and forbidden ecstasy, against the tree. She prayed to it that the wolf's seed would not implant itself and affect her potential offspring. The wolf plunged its long and dextrous tongue into her depths and still stimulated her clitoris, at the same time, bringing her to a drenched and tainted orgasm. She moaned and moaned, as the wolf's monstrous tongue pleasured her to new heights. He rocked his head back and forth, so his cold, wet nose rubbed against her genitalia, now, swollen with excitement.

She couldn't resist the urge to push her

buttocks out, and press down. So, the wolf's tongue slid deeper inside her and touched new, and unexplored, depths. She bounced up and down on it and felt the wolf respond, bobbing its head in rhythm to her. The wolf stimulated her to frenzy, such that she began to lose her footing and found herself hugging the tree, as she moved on the wolf. She felt him begin to rise and grip her legs, pulling her up, as he stood. She knew he was going to enter her.

She felt her skin scuff against the tree, as he slammed her hard, from behind, and howled. Aurora cried out in ecstasy, as his massive member throbbed and expanded inside her, igniting her entire being. She'd never felt anything so large and hot inside her. He caused new sensations to course through her. She screamed a new release, as she clenched her walls and gushed all over him, while he thrust in and out of her, pushing her hard, against the tree. She pushed back and rubbed herself, against him, bringing herself to a quarry of multiple orgasms, as the friction stimulated her. Her walls fought against his ever-expanding erection, as his excitement grew. She knew they were near their limit. She strained, as he stretched her legs further apart and delved deeper into her. He had hold of both of her legs, in a firm, faultless grip, and moved her up and down on him, as he thrust in and out of her so fast she couldn't keep up, but screamed in unison with his howls of triumph. She released a new stream of wetness over him, allowing him to expand further inside her. Large, as the wolf was, she now consumed the entirety of him and she was enjoying every massive inch of him. Aurora bucked in rhythm with the wolf's powerful thrusts, her elfish strength improving the sensations for both of them.

As she finished cumming over his hot and bulbous penis, the wolf placed her feet to the floor and humped over her. He banged her hard, against the tree, licking in her ear. As he thrust hard and fast, into her, crushing her harder, against the tree, she felt winded. So, she delicately guided him into a crouch, as she knelt on all fours, with him still inside her. He finished her, on all fours, in true doggy style. She pushed back, as he reached even greater depths, and all of him disappeared inside of her. She arched her back and pushed back, against his thrusts, as she squirted all over him. She wriggled, from side to side, and the wolf thrust her with new vigour, she screamed a pleasured response. He howled his release, as his final thrust released a huge rush of hot fluid inside her. He was off of her and fell asleep, before she had time to realize what had just transpired between them. She stood, immediately, and the wolf's juices gushed out of her. She ran to the river and bathed, begging her goddess that his seed would not plant itself in her womb.

As she ran back, out of the water, she fell to her knees, placed her head on the floor, and covered it with her hands. The wolf caught her scent and woke, suddenly. He jumped up and sprang on top of her, entering her from behind, causing her to jump up, onto her hands and scream in shock and pleasure. As the wolf thrust himself in and out of her, again, he was on all fours, bent over her. His thrusts were frantic and powerful, his member massive and throbbing, and still expanding. She spread her legs further, pushed her face down, between her elbows, and rose up and down, in rhythm, to accommodate him, but she was soon soaking him with her juices, and he slid deeper inside of her, until she had engulfed all of him. They both let out a cry of ecstasy, as he did so. He felt her contracting and she felt his throbbing member bring her to another orgasm.

The wolf leaned right over her and poked his head under her body. He reached out, with his long, slimy, wet tongue, and flicked her clitoris. She began to buck against him, uncontrollably. He slowed, to a gentle lap, and she rubbed up and down, on him, pushing her backside against him with all her strength. He gradually quickened his pace and felt her climax on him. His warm, wet release caused her to scream, as it over flowed and spurted out of her. Her depths were full when he withdrew.

Constellina leaped on the wolf, from behind. She leaned all of her weight to the side and clung on, as they tumbled over. She lost her sword in the sprawl. She was helpless. The wolf had her on her back, pinned down. She had her legs spread, either side of him and drew them back, reading herself to push him off. Before she could react, though, the wolf had plunged himself forward, inside of her, ripping through her garments, as he did so. She let out a violent scream.

"Don't fight, that's all he wants," Aurora shouted at her. "Don't panic my love, it's alright."

With that, Constellina relaxed as the wolf reached down and lapped at her dark pink genitalia. It swelled and moistened, as he rubbed it firm, against her. He thrust himself fully, in and out of her, bringing her closer and closer to climax with each stroke.

As the wolf thrust, Constellina rose to meet him, pushing back against his firm thrusts, and enjoying his large, flat tongue stimulate all of her at once. As she writhed against him, she felt him expanding inside of her, increasing the pace of his laps and thrusts, as she felt him grow hotter and throb against her. The sensation brought a rush of warmth to her genitals, inside and out. As he felt her clench and the rush of her warm juices all over his massive throbbing member, he howled, as he expelled his seed inside her in a warm throbbing release. Her walls had stretched to their limit and she cried out, as she clenched them down, over him for a final time. He pushed further into her, as he slumped against her. He gave a large yawn and fell asleep on top of her, his enormous penis still inside her. She felt filled to the brim. The aftermath of their sordid activity gushed out of her, as she pushed him out of her and slid from under him. He barely stirred in his sleep. She stood and went to bathe in the river, as had her lover, and prayed.

"Oh, my love." Aurora ran to join her in the cool, clear waters of the moonlit river. They embraced under the stars, as they soothed each other, after the shock of what had just happened sank in.

"We can't leave him, it's too dangerous," Constellina considered.

"Well, at least now we know what he wants in that state. We can keep him occupied and hopefully, satisfied enough not to inflict danger on anyone, until we can get him back to his Kingdom." Aurora suggested.

"Yes, quite. We can escort him back. Then, he will be safe. I just hope his wolf seed has not planted itself within us."

They exchanged a concerned look as Constellina spoke these words. To their surprise, the Prince had joined them, in his human form. He told the story of how he came to be a werewolf. He was attacked, one night. He was caught out late hunting.

"The King demanded I be locked away, in the deepest depths of the castle dungeons, each full moon. He would leave me a cow, or a pig, to feast upon, and I would be released, bloody and shamed, at sunrise. He considers me an abomination."

The Prince hung his head, as he spoke the words. The elf maids took pity and surrounded him, naked, in the water. As Aurora and Constellina embraced him, from in front and behind, he felt himself grow, between Aurora's legs. She inclined to his response by gently rubbing her slippery thighs back and forth, over his penis, smiling, as she did so. She reached forward and kissed him hard. Constellina knelt behind him, running her finger nails down his back, causing him to jolt and shudder. As she knelt in the shallow water, she cupped his balls, one in each hand, and began to lick them, Aurora still thrust over his penis. Stimulating her clitoris, she began to moan. She felt her partner's familiar finger sliding in and out her gapping vagina. She was drenched. As she rubbed harder and faster, over the Prince's penis, and Constellina thrust her fingers deeper in and out of her, she came and squirted all over the Prince, who's tip inched its way inside of her, as his sexual excitement increased and his member grew. Aurora, overcome with arousal, leaped onto the Prince's penis, wrapping herself around him, and she began bouncing herself up and down on him, groaning with pleasure, as she did so. The Prince gripped onto her and began thrusting back, against her, Constellina still stimulating him, as she did so. As Aurora came all over him, her juices dripping down his legs, she slid off him and under her lover.

Aurora pulled Constellina's lips apart and licked her tongue, hard, over her, causing her to gasp. She positioned herself over Aurora's beautiful face and rubbed herself all over it, feeling her tongue stimulate her to ecstasy. Constellina dripped down Aurora's throat, as she became more excited, squirting into her mouth. Aurora took three of her long, slender fingers and inserted them deep into her lover's depths, causing her to gasp and suck in her breath, releasing it, as she stimulated her cervix. Aurora felt Constellina clenching over her finger, she wiggled them more vigorously, inside her, in response. Constellina writhed more furiously over her partner's face and the volume of her groans increased, as Aurora brought her to a powerful climax. She felt her juices gush out of her as she finished. Aurora's face was wet with her lover's orgasmic aftermath.

The sight of the two women had stimulated the Prince to a hard and throbbing erection, which he was caressing with both his hands. Constellina knelt before him and spread her legs. She looked at him, over her shoulder, with an unmistakable intention in her eye and a half smile on her face. She wiggled her buttocks at him expectantly. The excitement overcame the Prince, once again, and she looked in horror, as he began to transform, again. His penis swelled before her eyes, as it came rushing towards her and slammed inside her with a fierce jolt. The pressure caused her to leap up and scream in response, as she felt him fill every bit of her. He was deep, deep inside her, as he stimulated her depths from behind. He was on all fours, driving down hard on her. As he drove down, upon her she stuck her buttocks high into the air and rose up, to meet him, taking in all of him with every thrust. He leaned over and stimulated her clitoris with his tongue, as he quickened his pace inside her and she felt him expanding. She became wetter and wetter, as her excitement increased. Her clitoris continued to swell and the feeling rose from deep inside her, and spread throughout her body. She felt an overwhelming release, as she came and felt the wolf expand for a final time. He released a gush inside her, driving himself down, upon her, harder still. She buckled beneath him, in the release. He went down with her, on top of her, still inside her, as he drove himself to a hard finish. She lay gasping, as he withdrew. Her walls were clearly stretched, as they hung, while his juices gushed out of her. They were all spent.

8 THE PRINCE PART 3
The Pixie

The Prince and the elves had been travelling for over seven sun rises and sunsets since the last full moon had passed. The arduous journey was beginning to take its toll. They needed a rest and a relief, soon. They found a small clearing concealed by a circle of large, aged oak trees and the predecessors' remains. The Prince informed the elves that he had spotted a herd of deer heading in their direction and would like to go hunting for food. Although their physical capability far surpassed the Prince's and this would have been much easier for them, the elves did not object, grateful for the opportunity to have some time alone together. As the Prince wandered off in to the forest, they lay down their luggage and began to undress. Unbeknown to them, during the last day of their journey, they had acquired an unexpected companion, who crouched watching them strip to their skin through the confines of a hollowed old oak trunk.

The creature gasped in a high-pitched squeak as the elves revealed every curve and crevice of their beauty, the creature witnessed with a sense of awe. She felt startled again as she saw the two elfin maids embrace and exchange a series of passionate kisses. The creature's excitement grew as their wandering hands danced to tuneful whimpers of pleasure. The creature felt tingles running up and down its spine in unison as the elves stroked up and down each others' beautiful bodies. They stroked their way down and as they stood and placed their hands between each others' legs and rested them for a moment in the crevice just before their lush, swollen lips. They were both so sensitive they panted as they brushed over each other, sending shivering sensations down their spines. As the elves teased around the outer regions of their womanhoods, they kissed and gasped in rhythm. The creature watched with intent, feeling her own genitalia growing moist and excited with anticipation; she did not resist the urge to reach down to her smooth, naked crotch and follow the elves motion, and she was careful to stay quiet, not that it would have mattered at the volume the elves were now vocalising. They parted each others' lips simultaneously and cried out in unison as they touched their expectant clitoris. They felt waves of pleasure rush through them as they drew themselves closer and rubbed over each other. The creature parted her own lips and felt a rush of wetness leak out of her as she fought to contain an excited gasp. The elves hands were moving frantically all over their nether regions, one moment fingers sliding out of squirting vaginas, the next rubbing furiously over swollen mounds, the excitement building. The creature rubbed herself as she watched; she had never felt such arousal before, or even dreamt that such an act would ever be witnessed by the likes of her, a mere pixie.

The elves moved to the floor and dived head first in to each others' genitals. Constellina was on top and lapped at Aurora's juices, making intense groaning sounds as she rubbed herself over Aurora's face and tongue, the vibrations coming from Aurora stimulated her even more and likewise for Aurora as she felt her own stimulation increase with Constellina's. The elves lapped and groaned over each other, drinking every drop of their sexual arousal. Their fingers slipped in and out of each other so fast it was a daze to watch. They could feel each other clenching harder and were thrusting faster. The elves thrust and rubbed themselves to an orgasmic oblivion, Constellina on top and Aurora beneath her. They jiggled and jerked as they squirted all over each other to an intense and satisfied finish. The pixie did the same; she fought to contain an orgasmic shriek of pleasure but failed, the elves looked up immediately, startled by the sudden sound.

Realising she'd blown her cover, the naked pixie emerged, fluttering above the trunk in which she was hiding. Her magnificent blue butterfly wings spanned more than twice her body length but appeared thinner and more penetrable than paper. The reflective sheen caught and bounced the light off of them all around the clearing as she hovered above the trunk. She was a beautiful sight for any unexpected creature to lay eyes on, though she did not realise it. The elves leant down to reach for their weapons.

"No, please! I meant no harm!" The pixie threw the words at them in panicked alarm. Physically, she would be no match for an elf woman, but with the advantage of flight and little pixie tricks, she was a potential threat.

Aurora was first to respond.

"Then why, oh little-blue-winged-one, do you lay cowering in a rotten tree trunk, spying on us like an indecent perverted goblin girl?" Her voice was firm and questioning. A red flush filled the pixie's cheeks, turning her purple. She looked down and crossed her arms straight over in front of her. She was completely naked and her perfect, pert little breasts had the elf maiden's eyes wandering. She pointed downward and indicated the small trail of orgasmic aftermath that still trailed down the inside of her thighs.

"Something not too dissimilar to what you were up to, by the sounds of it," she responded sarcastically. A small, dirty smirk wrote itself across her face and she said,

"You know, you can always use a pair of extra hands in these situations."

"We do not require any more hands, thank you very much. We believed we were alone together, for once. We're on a treacherous journey to return something of great value to the King."

"You mean his son," the pixie interjected, drawing herself up higher and moving closer towards the elves and the clearing. Her beauty took their breath away, if only for a split-second.

"Yes, I know of this, I've been following

you for longer than you realise. Don't worry, your secret is safe with me," she smirked at them again, "I just ask that, well, let's say the asking is just for niceties, but I ask that you let me join you for the rest of your journey, and I promise I will make myself, quite, useful," as she continued she fluttered over to the still naked elves and angled herself so that her wings fluttered against their still excited womanhoods. They both clutched at them and turned in shock and gasped with embarrassment at their sudden and inappropriate arousal. The pixie swept back and forth beneath them both tickling her wings over the elves bodies until they succumbed. As they felt themselves growing wetter and more aroused, they found they couldn't help but finally lay themselves down in the thicket, and let her ravage them with her wings.

The pixie laid a wing tip against each elf and drew it back gently over their most sensitive area. They whispered little shrieks of pleasure as they tilted their heads back and relaxed on to the pixie's wings. The pixie fluttered her wings over the elves at the speed of hummingbird's wings. As she heard the elves gasps grow louder and morph in to moans, they felt waves of pleasure course through them. The pixie pressed harder, increasing the pressure against them. She felt the elves writhing over her wings and she paused briefly to turn and face them.

She resumed her fluttering and witnessed the result oozing from the girls' aroused womanhoods and watched it trickle down in to the crevice between their legs. She felt her own juices flow as she experienced and overwhelming desire to taste it. She licked her lips. Starting with Aurora, she leant forward and inserted her tongue deep inside her and moved it around against Aurora's walls. Aurora cried out and thrust on to her as she felt herself respond. Her walls contracted over the pixie's tongue, they both felt it. The pixie, still fluttering her wings, took two of her fingers and wiped them around the outside of Constellina's wet and writhing womanhood, and she slipped them inside her and felt her clench down on them immediately and cry out. The pixie thrust in and out of the elves with her fingers and tongue, alternating between them as she continued to flutter her beautiful blue wings over their clitorises. Over and over, she brought the beautiful elf maids, legs spread, holes wide open, to a decadent and unexplored ecstasy. The elves saturated the world around them with the aftermath of their continuous sexual stimulation.

The pixie grew bored of this and turned to Aurora. She fluttered so that she lay hovering over her, her boobs in Aurora's face. Aurora cupped them in her hands, she covered them both with ease, the pixie was tiny by comparison, but what she lacked in size, she made up for in energy and enthusiasm. She grasped Aurora's face and drew it towards her, kissing her passionately as she slid herself over the elf's still spread legs. She wrapped herself over the elf so that their genitalia made contact, and, using her wings, propelled herself furiously up and down over Aurora's still wet womanhood, stimulating her to another orgasm. As Aurora screamed her pleasure, the pixie shot down and began to lick furiously over her clitoris. She licked everywhere: up, down, in, out, in circles, in waves, in flicks and strokes, any way to make Aurora moan over and over.

Constellina grew increasingly excited, and as she watched her partner, she couldn't resist reaching down and rubbing herself, feeling the tell-tale signs drip out of her as her arousal became apparent. As the pixie brought Aurora to another orgasm with her tongue, she could stand by and watch no more. She leapt over to the pixie, grasping her legs with her hands, and she assertively pulled her legs apart and delved her tongue inside her tiny hole, and she felt it expand immediately. The pixie screamed and began to bounce, pushing herself down on it. Constellina swiped it over the pixie's tiny, dark blue clitoris and inserted two of her fingers inside her. She felt her tight walls soon give way to a drenched and slippery mess as her sexual arousal heightened.

It wasn't long before Constellina felt Aurora's familiar hands and other body parts reach round and guide her bottom half on to her own fingers and tongue. The elves and the pixie lay in a triangle formation, stimulating one another to a delightful ecstasy over and over as they plunged fingers and tongues in and out of each other while they moaned and groaned themselves to orgasmic pleasure.

The Prince had returned and had stopped short of the clearing as he heard the three female creatures engaged in a passionate array of sexual activity. He approached cautiously and stopped when he witnessed the beautiful sight through a gap in the undergrowth. He remained unseen. As he continued to watch the three women pleasure each other, he felt his arousal growing in to an uncomfortable bulge, fighting its restraints. He dropped his kill and bow and arrows to the ground, along with his garments. He reached down and grasped his hard penis in both hands and stimulated himself. He felt his excitement grow as the women shifted position. His enjoyment increased as he watched the elf women stand and lift the pixie by her ankles. They continued to pleasure her with their fingers and tongues as they raised her off the ground. She dangled before them and was just the right length to reach in to them, one with each hand, and pleasure them both as she cried out. The Prince increased his rhythmic movement as his pleasure increased at the sight. He felt a pull in his loins indicating the excitement was almost enough to cause him to explode, and he reduced his speed to a gentle up and down motion; he wanted to enjoy this for a little longer.

The elves turned the pixie upright. She fluttered to stay at eye level with them, her toes dangled just below their knees. They took it in turns to kiss and stimulate one another, fingers darting in and out as they writhed against each other. The pixie vocalised an intense orgasm, her juices flowing from her, all over Aurora's hand. Aurora curled her hand in to a small fist, and pressed it against the pixie; she felt the pixie clench over her and she waited for her to relax before increasing the pressure and inserting her fist further inside her. The pixie spread her legs wide apart and lowered herself further on to Aurora's straining fist, screaming as she did so. Aurora continued to force her fist upwards, slowly feeling it engulfed by the pixie's clenching walls, and she watched it disappear. The pixie let out another scream as she felt Aurora's entire fist slip inside her, and she began to wriggle on it, vocalising as Aurora plunged deep inside her.

Aurora felt her partner's familiar tongue flicking over her clitoris and waves of pleasure rushed through her. Constellina slipped four of her fingers inside Aurora's vacant vagina and felt her engulf them immediately. She brought her thumb round and inserted it as well, expanding her hand inside Aurora as she fought her way inside. Aurora pushed down and wiggled, vocalising her encouragement as she took Constellina's whole hand inside her. As Aurora's own excitement grew, she fisted the pixie fast and furiously, bouncing her up and down as she fluttered in mid-air, her legs spread far apart. She was still incredibly tight, and Aurora's hand did not move much as she contracted over it again and again in waves of orgasmic ecstasy. The pixie was drenched and could feel her excitement rising from deeper within her. She cried out as the rush overwhelmed her and bucked herself furiously over Aurora's fist as she came. Aurora slid further inside her as the pixie's walls relaxed. Constellina delved in and out of Aurora's depth, all the while flicking her tongue over her swollen clitoris, until she felt Aurora's juices flow out of her and soak her arm. Aurora felt the release as Constellina brought her to another climax and let out a loud sigh as she relaxed to a finish, withdrawing her hand from the pixie's deep blue depths.

The Prince startled to a stop as he heard another male voice sigh to the side of him. He turned to look and saw a very large and lean, yet powerfully built elf-man, raised a finger to his lips and hold up his other hand to indicate his presence was harmless, and he did not wish to interrupt the show. As if to prove this further, the elf-man stripped naked before the Prince and reached for his still soft penis. The Prince was in awe, and he was aware that he was a very well-endowed man, but even soft, the elf-man's penis appeared to be mocking him by comparison. Still soft, it hung low past his testicles and a good few inches down his thighs. Its girth appeared thicker soft than he was erect. The Prince, for the first time in his life, felt conscious of his apparent lack of size, in all respects. The elf-man was over a good half foot taller than the Prince, and as the Prince watched in shock as his penis rose and pointed towards him, he appeared almost menacing. Whenever the Prince thought that the elf-man must be fully erect, he just watched him keep on growing. Even clasping it in both hands, he still didn't cover half his length, and even the elf-man's large hands were not large enough to wrap around it fully. The elf-man stared at the women with a look of intent in his eye, and the Prince continued to stare at the elf-man. As he gazed, the elf-man eventually turned to him and said,

"Curious, are you? Well, who wouldn't be?" He walked over to the Prince and, before he could register what was happening, grasped his penis in his large, angular hand, in a grip so firm the Prince gasped, and began to stroke up and down his shaft. The Prince, still consumed with shock, mimicked the elf-man's actions, causing him to release a pleasurable sigh. The Prince's shock increased as the elf-man began to move back and forth in rhythm to the Prince's strokes, releasing barely audible rumbles from his throat. The Prince did the same in to the elf-man's hand and found himself releasing deep grunts of pleasure as he did so. The two men stood rocking back and forth against one another. One hand over each penis, they felt their stimulation increase as they turned to watch the women in the clearing continue to bring themselves to an intense erotic ecstasy.

9 THE PRINCE PART 4
The Elf Man

The Prince felt his sexual excitement rushing up through him, about to reach his peak. Before the release found him, the Prince felt the elf-man kneel down before him and take his penis in his mouth; he swallowed the Prince all the way down to his testicles with ease. The Prince felt the vibrations in the elf-man's throat bring him to an intense orgasm, and he felt himself ejaculate down his throat. The elf-man stood and the Prince exchanged places. He knelt before the elf-mans penis, and he was even more aware of its size, unable to comprehend how he would be able to swallow it down; as the elf-man had done his own, he continued to stroke it and lick up and down his shaft.

Having lubricated it a bit with his saliva, he popped the tip inside his mouth and licked its sensitive part. The elf-man rumbled and thrust towards him, indicating he wished the Prince to take more of him inside. The Prince widened his jaw as far as it would go and strained to fit as much of the elf-man in his mouth as he could. The elf-man felt the Prince's resistance over his massive girth and his sexual excitement exploded out of him and filled the Prince, causing him to gulp as he felt the warm rush at the back of his throat. The Prince stood and faced the elf-man, wiping his chin as he did so; he watched his own seed trickle from the corner of the elf-man's lips as he smiled,

"Now, to tend to the women," he informed the Prince as he turned to face them. The Prince noticed the elf-man was soft again as he wandered off towards the three screaming women. He looked down and his own erection still remained, ah-ha, there must be some disadvantages to having one that size, he concluded and immediately felt better.

The women turned and gave the elf a confused look as he strode towards them,

"Ladies, I do apologise if I am interrupting anything here, but looks like you wouldn't mind some assistance."

The women swooned at the sight of him;

he was a huge, fine example of a man for any species, even more so than the Prince, and they couldn't help but notice the equipment he carried was magnificent. He had long blonde hair and masculine, chiselled features. Solid as stone and perfectly proportional, the naked elf-man turned to the pixie girl. He clasped her tiny, delicate chin between his massive fingers, looked down upon her and smiled. Even still soft, he appeared massive by comparison, and she wondered if he would ever fit inside her. She wanted to know how big he would be. She leant forward and began to lick up and down the elf-man's soft shaft, as it hung limp between his legs. Standing, she only stood a head above his genitals. She cupped his enormous balls, nearly the size of her breasts, in her hands and felt the elf-man begin to grow.

At first, he remained pointing downwards, and she felt him swell and, already massive, his manhood protruded outward. She watched herself gliding over and over him, taking longer to reach from end to end with each stroke. His breathing increased as he started to rise. She grasped the tip in her mouth as he did so and rose herself up with him. He was ginormous, as long and big around as the pixie's forearm, and they were all sure he would destroy her. The pixie continued to attempt to slide her mouth over the end of the elf-man's penis. She reached forward to grasp it and found that she was unable to touch her finger tips together by over a thumbs breadth. She slid both her hands over elf-man's penis, causing him to rumble a deep groan of satisfaction.

He opened his eyes and looked down at her, picked her up and sat her over his face, holding her with only one hand as she fluttered to steady herself. She wrapped her legs around the elf-man's head and writhed over his face as she felt his enormous tongue sliding in and out and over her. He took his other hand and rubbed it over her leaking vagina. His middle finger was almost the same size as a male pixie's penis, so when he slid it inside of her, the pixie gasped with fulfilled pleasure at the penetration. She felt her walls contracting over it furiously as he brought her to an intense and sodden orgasm.

The elf-man brought the pixie down over him; she felt him reach beneath her and was surprised when she felt him rub a soft penis over her. He lubricated himself with her juices and popped it inside of her. Even soft he filled her tiny depths, he circled his penis around inside her, and she moved in rhythm, groaning a pleasurable response as she felt him grow firmer and bigger as she did so. She yelped as he began to force her apart, and she couldn't help but spread her legs wider and relax open and on to him. As she felt him straining against her walls and filling her depths, he slid himself deeper inside of her. She spread her legs as far apart as possible to compensate. She felt her hole pulling back against the elf-man's penis and waves of pleasure rose over him.

The elf-man enjoyed feeling himself grow inside the tiny pixie girl and watching her pleasured response as he did so. Even soft she felt tight against him, and as he grew, he felt her walls physically constrict against his penis, the firm pressure sent sensations through him and he felt himself grow warm and feel the urge to move with the waves of pleasure coursing through him.

He held her legs apart and thrust in and out of her; he was so big inside her now she could feel him stimulate places she didn't even know existed, and she felt as though he had reached her centre as the waves of pleasure ran through her continuously. He continued to pull her on to him, delving deeper as he continued to grow. She felt his tip reach her bottom and stroke over it, sending orgasmic waves up through her and she tilted her head back and screamed. He bounced her up and down on him and heard the rhythm of his thrusts as his ginormous member plunged in and out of her tiny frame. He enjoyed the view, with her legs splayed and leaning back, and she exposed all of herself to him. He took in her beauty and rubbed his hands all over her body and rubbed her clitoris as he brought her to a sensational orgasm.

The pixie couldn't get enough of the ginormous elf-man inside her, thrusting his ginormous member in and out of unexplored depths, and she felt feelings she hadn't known existed. She enjoyed the increased friction as she felt her walls stretch to accommodate his ever growing member. She felt him have to force his way back in to her every time he pulled out, feeling her contracting over him. As he felt her contractions increase in strength and speed as she came, he fought to control himself and pulled out of her. He wanted this build up to last and wanted to take his time enjoying a powerful finish. He placed the pixie girl on her hands and knees in front of him. He got down on all fours on top of her, and he took a hand to part her lips and began thrusting his middle finger in and out of her and sliding his thumb over her clitoris. She pushed back on to him and moved in rhythm and felt herself tremble as she reached another writhing orgasm. The elf-man felt her drip all over his hand

and her vagina relax and took his chance. He pushed her down and pulled her buttocks up towards him, and he parted her lips and placed the tip of his penis against them. The girth of his massive penis was wider than the pixie's gaping hole, even when pulled apart. He aimed the tip and inserted it inside her inch by inch. He felt her fighting her contracting walls to let him in. He felt the friction fighting his entry as he increased his force and plunged himself inside her. She screamed and pushed herself on to him. He felt the skin of his shaft pulled back and her walls stimulate his excitement immediately.

He began to thrust himself in and out of her and felt her push back. The view was magnificent as he witnessed his ginormous member sliding in and out of the tiny pixie girl's expanding hole. At first, he was only able to enter half of his member inside her, but as she writhed and pushed back on to him further and further, he watched himself disappearing. With each stroke back, he pushed further forward in to her and held the end of her depths drawing deeper inside her. He was over three quarters of the way in now. He grasped her buttocks and guided her over him, pressing down harder until he saw his entire shaft disappear and felt the beautiful soft skin of her buttocks brush against him. He increased the speed and strength of his thrusts, causing her to howl with intense pleasure and slid his thumb over her clitoris. He felt the pixie girl squirting over his now fully erect manhood. She was so tight he felt as if he was squeezing himself inside her with every thrust. She felt a magnitude of sensations she thought was not possible.

The elf-man leaned over the pixie as he felt himself drawing closer to his powerful finish. He slammed in and out of her, pushing her backwards and forwards with the force of his thrusts. She felt waves of contractions flow out from her centre and released a loud scream of pleasure as she felt the elf-man throb and expand further inside her and the hot rush as his juices filled and stung her friction burned vaginal walls. The elf grunted a deep, rumbling groan of pleasure as he felt himself release inside her.

He leant over the pixie, and she pulled away from him and lay face down on the floor. Constellina wandered over to him, and she grasped his face in her hands and drew him in to a passionate kiss and slid herself underneath him. She wrapped her legs around his hips and drew herself up on to him,

"Take me." She gasped. The elf-man responded and slid himself deep inside the elfin maid with ease, her proportions much more accommodating for him. He felt himself swell inside her as her dripping vagina engulfed him and she rose to meet him, rubbing against him and releasing breathless gasps as she writhed. The elf-man felt his excitement pull in his loins and rush up through his body in response. He plunged himself deeper in to the elfin maid and, without due care, pushed and pulled her over him as he thrust hard in to her. The sound echoed through the forest, and the elves solid bodies bashed against each other hard and fast. Their vocalisations a faint background noise by comparison. Constellina wailed and writhed as the elf-man's ginormous penis brought her to intense finish. He felt her walls contract over him and the tightness caused him to release a load inside her. He withdrew and lay spent beside her. She rocked backwards immediately in an attempt to engulf his seed.

The Prince emerged from the forest, naked and hard, dragging his kill beside him. The three women stared at him, and the pixie fluttered her wings and hovered above the ground. The prince thought she looked shy and embarrassed at the sight of his protruding penis as he lay his kill and weapons down beside her.

"No need to fear little one, my intentions are for your enjoyment only," he cupped the pixies tiny face in his hands and pulled her towards him until their lips locked. The pixie responded as she felt the Prince's soft kiss excite her and wrapped her arms around him. She still felt moist and gaping from her encounter with the elf-man, his seed still dripping from her. She slid herself down and on to the Prince's penis, guiding him inside her. They both released a gasp as he slid inside her with difficulty. The Prince, although not as big as the elf-man, still struggled to fit himself inside her tiny hole. She felt tight as he felt the skin of his shaft pulled back as he fought to fill her depths. She moaned as he reached her centre and she felt waves of pleasure flow from it.

Constellina moved behind the Prince and knelt down. She reached up and grasped his testicles in her hands; she leant forward and licked them. The Prince felt a tingling sensation run up through him, and he pulled back. His tip met no resistance when he pushed forwards again, but he felt the pixie grow tight and constrict over his shaft. They both pushed firmly against one another until it slid all the way inside her, her legs spreading as it went, until she engulfed him.

Aurora approached Constellina from behind and crouched down on all fours and began to lick her still swollen clitoris. Seeing Aurora bent over, with her beautiful bottom pointing skywards, and her depths exposed, he could not resist. He crawled over behind Aurora and slammed himself inside her with ease. He thrust in and out of her and felt her push back against him.

The pixie gasped as the Prince plunged in and out of her and began to writhe over him. The Prince moaned deep and proud as he felt his penis throb with excitement as the tiny pixie's tight blue walls sent waves of pure pleasure coursing through him. He moved back against her, thrusting in and out of her as she fluttered her wings and writhed, lifting herself on and off him. She tightened her grip over his penis and quickened her pace. She panted excited little gasps as she grew more excited. The Prince felt her squirt all over him and felt himself expand and throb deep inside her. All of her was constricting over his penis so hard he felt himself explode inside her as he pulled her down hard on to him. He cried out his release and she squeaked hers.

Behind them, Aurora brought Constellina to an intense orgasm with her fingers and tongue. Constellina screamed and leant forward as she finished and squirted in Aurora's face. Aurora bent down as Constellina pulled away and pushed back harder and moaned louder as the excited elf-man thrust in and out of her, harder and faster. The pixie slid herself underneath Aurora, burying her face in her womanhood as the elf continued to penetrate her. The pixie lapped at Aurora's juices over her clitoris and heard her scream an ecstatic response. The elf-man felt Aurora grow tight and pulsate over his penis as she came more intense than before. He felt his own pleasure well up and flow out of him. He leant over her as he grunted a finish.

The Prince walked over and kneeled behind Aurora next to the elf-man, each took a leg and pulled it further apart, and guided her buttocks up to meet their tips. The elf-man went first; he took his finger tips and placed them either side of her vagina and pulled it apart that it stretched with ease. The pixie continued to stimulate Aurora's clitoris, and she moaned and gushed juices all over the elf-man's hands. He took his tip and pushed it inside her with ease, then let the rest of him follow. He moved in and out of her and placed a little finger inside her, running it around the edge of her vagina, stretching it further apart as he did so. He then took his middle finger, and his index; all the while, Aurora was brought to multiple orgasms by the pixie's flicking.

The Prince saw his cue and placed his tip against Aurora's vagina; she responded and relaxed open, revealing space for the Prince to enter. He pushed against her as the elf-man pulled her walls over to one side. It was so tight in there and Aurora howled like an animal. He pushed hard against Aurora, and the elf-mans penis, and felt them both resist. He moved in and out a few times, but without much progress. Constellina was by his side and grasped his penis and slid it inside her mouth. She dribbled and soaked it with her saliva, her hand slid easily over his sopping wet penis as she pulled on it. Constellina guided the Prince back to Aurora, and this time, he watched himself slide in with greater ease, still feeling an intense constriction as he plunged further inside. Aurora's response was frantic. She bucked and writhed furiously, pushing herself back and forth on to both men's members. They took it in turns to plunge in and out of Aurora, who felt a constant conflicting sensation against her walls which contracted faster and more intense than ever before. As the pixie pushed her tongue flat over her clitoris and rubbed furiously over it Aurora was brought to a series of multiple orgasms so intense that her screeches of pleasure startled animals in the surrounding undergrowth. Birds, rabbits, deer and mice fled from the immediate area. Aurora squirted over the men's penises and the pixie's face. Both men slid all the way down deep inside her as they finished.

The two men laid on their backs side by side to rest. They were still erect, and the two elf women straddled them, guiding their penises inside their hot wet vaginas, releasing a gasp as they engulfed them. The pixie fluttered over and sat on the elf-man's face. She let him bring her to orgasm with his fingers and tongue and then fluttered over to the Prince. Aurora and Constellina rose up and down on the elf-man and the Prince, moaning and writhing as they did so. The feelings of pleasure rose through them every time they sat down harder. The men felt themselves expanding inside the beautiful elves' tight, wet vaginas. Aurora and Constellina felt the pleasure well up and out of them, and they increased their pace as they felt the release wash over them. The men released orgasmic groans as they felt their own release leave them and fill the women. The pixie was still alternating over the elf-man and the Prince, her orgasms increasing in intensity. The elfin maids lay on their backs with their legs up. The elf-man and the Prince hung limp and lifeless, now truly spent.

"Right enough of this," Constellina

called. The pixie stopped writhing over the elf-man's face and flew up, "it is time we make way, we cannot afford to delay any longer," she continued.

"Where, may I ask, my dear lady, are you going?" The elf-man spoke in a firm and polite tone.

"We are escorting his royal highness, the Prince of Fantastica, to his kingdom to reunite him with his father. We left the battle to the West nearly half a lunar cycle's time ago. We are well half way to our destination now," Constellina informed him.

"Well, I was just heading in that direction myself. Don't mind if I join you." He smiled at them all, making it clear it was not a question.

"You are all welcome to join us for the rest of our journey as long as you do not jeopardise our safety or make a nuisance of yourself," she glanced at the pixie. They all nodded and gathered the clothes and belongings, preparing to set off to continue their journey. The Prince and the elfin maids were aware that it was unlikely they would reach the Kingdom before the next lunar cycle, and it concerned them.

10 THE PRINCE PART 5
The Pole

They wandered on for another day and a half without rest, but exhaustion finally forced them to take a pause next to a stream. They collected water, ate a meal, and laid down to rest next to the trickling water. Constellina was the first to initiate the activity. She took Aurora's waist and drew her towards her in a fierce embrace. The two elfin maids exchanged tongues and their hands wandered. Constellina stripped Aurora who reciprocated, wandering hands finding expectant clitorises. They panted and gasped as they felt tingling sensations rush up through them. Their vaginas became wet and their clitorises swelled. Constellina reached into her bag and pulled out what could only be described as a double length, elf-penis-shaped object.

Constellina took the pole and licked it, coating it with a thick layer of saliva from her tongue at one end, and inserted it in to her partner's gaping wet vagina. Aurora gasped as the cold, slimy, phallic object breached the walls of her hungry orifice. She clamped down on it involuntarily as the act of penetration brought her to an almighty climax. Constellina leapt down upon her and wrapped her tongue around her clitoris too fast for the human eye, and within seconds, she had brought Aurora to a climactic state as she writhed and moaned on the forest floor with her legs spread wide and her juices gushing beneath them both.

As she writhed until she could writhe no more, Constellina took it upon herself to stimulate her to near climax and then stop. As she brought Aurora to a finish, she turned and planted herself on to Aurora's face. She sat up and took hold of the pole and began thrusting it in to Aurora over and over. Aurora moaned into Constellina's elfin depths, and the vibrations, coupled with the stimulation brought by Aurora's vigorous tongue movements, brought Constellina to reach an intense orgasm and quicken her thrusts in and out of Aurora's saturated depths. As the two elf women reached their climaxes, they released a final orgasmic groan.

The rest of the group watched, feeling their own stirrings of arousal start as they watched the two beautiful naked elfin maidens stimulate each other to an intense ecstasy. They relieved themselves of their garments and reached down for their genitals. They stroked themselves and then reached out with their other hand for each other. The pixie found the Prince, the Prince found the elf-man, and the elf-man plunged his huge finger inside the pixie's tiny opening and enjoyed watching her gasp as she engulfed it. They turned back to watch the elves in anticipation.

Constellina laid the pole on the floor in front of Aurora and crouched facing away from her on all fours. Aurora then manoeuvred herself on to all fours facing the opposite way. She reached under herself, stroking her clitoris as she did so and groaned with anticipation as it swelled. She took hold of the pole and aimed it in to Constellina's now expanded vagina, moist with anticipation. As Aurora inserted the pole in to Constellina, the elf woman gasped and sucked in her breath, and released a moan of pleasure as it sank in to her depths, now coated with her essence. Unable to resist the urge, Constellina backed up as far as she dared towards Aurora's beautiful bottom. As Aurora did the same, their cheeks met and both jolted in excitement at the contact. They let out an audible sigh as the pole moved inside them both, and Constellina began to buck and grind furiously up against Aurora's behind, crying out with pleasure as she did so. This in turn caused Aurora to respond by resisting in rhythm, and she let out long screams of intense pleasure as she felt Constellina moving up against her, causing the pole inside her to jolt up and down furiously hitting many sensitive spots inside her all at once.

"I want to see your beautiful bottom," Constellina paused to tell her. She slid off the pole and turned so she was facing Aurora's bottom. She began to stroke and play with it, taking in every detail as she gawped in admiration at her lover's beauty. She straddled the pole and crossed her legs under it and moved back and forward over it. She placed one hand behind and one on the small of Aurora's back and controlled the movement of the pole, in and out of Aurora's beautiful, aroused womanhood and back and forth over her swollen clitoris. As she continued, she moved over the pole herself, increasing the intensity of the stimulation, and she felt Aurora respond by moving over the pole in rhythm as she slid it in and out of her. She admired the view as she looked down upon her lover's perfect form. Her peach, full cheeks jiggled just the right amount as Aurora's motion stimulated them. She couldn't resist; she slid her hand down to grope them as she felt herself come over the pole as she penetrated her partner to another intense round of orgasms.

"Your turn," Aurora paused and spoke in a stern but sensual feminine tone. She guided her partner into position and slid under her, facing away from her. She inserted the pole into her partner's hot, wide and expectant womanhood as she made contact with her clitoris, giving it wet kisses at a furious pace. This was enough to excite Constellina to groan as it swelled in her mouth. Constellina thrust Aurora hard with the pole as she dragged her flattened tongue up and down over Aurora, and she heard her desperate pleas and whimpers for more, but Constellina continued to tease her, enjoying hearing her partner demand more. Aurora screamed at Constellina to continue as she started adding pauses to her placid routine.

"Don't stop! Oh no! No! Keep going! Never Stop!" She almost begged.

The elf-man was unable to contain his excitement at the sight and picked the pixie up on his finger, which was still inside her. He used a finger on his other hand to pull her apart. Realizing what he was doing, the pixie obliged and spread her legs wide as she could and yelped as she felt him push her down hard on to the tip of his ginormous manhood. He grunted as he felt himself touch her moist entrance.

Constellina adhered as she felt her partner growing tired of her teasing and finally sped up her motion and lapped her partner to a wet and wonderful round of intense multiple orgasms. She squirted over the pole as she clenched down, and Constellina continued to penetrate her hard as she pushed back to increase the intensity of the internal sensations she felt. She finished and slid off as she felt her partner's actions continue. She turned and smiled up at her,

"Fun as this is, we'll never conceive a child this way."

They both turned to look at the obliging elf-man, who pulled the pixie off him mid-orgasm, her screaming ceased immediately. He was ripe and ready to service them. They beckoned him over to them, and the elf-man knelt behind Constellina and slammed himself straight inside her. She cried out and tossed her head as she felt his massive member spread her depths wide open and fill them. She spread her legs wider to accommodate him. The elf-man rumbled a moan as he felt himself relax and expand as his pleasure increased. He grabbed hold of her buttocks and rammed himself in and out of her until he was overwhelmed with pleasure and cried out a loud masculine sigh as he released his seed inside Constellina. All the while, Constellina penetrated Aurora with the pole and her tongue, bringing her to climax.

The elf-man withdrew from Constellina, who stood and allowed Aurora to slide herself down and over the elf-man's still throbbing manhood. Despite his size, she slid over and engulfed him with ease and writhed over him releasing gasps of pleasure as he stimulated her insides to an intense climax. The elf-man took Aurora's toned yet shapely legs and pinned them behind her, opening her up wider, allowing him to lean forward and slide himself deeper inside her. She cried out as she felt him reach the bottom of her cavernous depths and stimulate them to an intense climax, contracting over the tip of his manhood. They both felt the waves of pleasure course through them as they began to move with one another, feeling the stimulation grow inside them. The elf-man slid in and out of Aurora deep and slow, each stroke bringing him closer and closer to satisfied finish. Aurora rose to meet him as he reached inside of her, feeling his massive girth against her contracting walls, filling her over and over. The elf-man took the pole and plunged it deep inside of her causing her to scream and thrust against it. The elf-man felt himself about to explode inside her, and he leaned over and rigorously thrust in and out, causing her to scream with ecstasy. He felt the release gush out of him as he filled her with his powerful seed. She clenched over his throbbing member, feeling orgasmic waves overwhelm her trembling body as he finished inside of her.

The pixie flew over and squashed her tiny, delicate frame and seemingly undersized hole on to the Prince's massive throbbing penis. She screamed as she fought to get him inside her. He was so big by comparison. Aurora rushed over and began stimulating her clitoris with her tongue, and with the Prince's guidance, he eased her down on to his massive throbbing penis. He was surprised when the tiny little pixie began hurling herself up and down on it; she spread so wide apart he feared she may split up the middle any second, but she appeared to be enjoying getting as much of him inside her as she could. He felt her, and himself, expanding with each stroke. She was so wet that there was little resistance now, despite her small size. The Prince felt his excitement grow within his penis and clasped the tiny pixie's beautiful buttocks and pulled her down on to him as he thrust himself inside her. She yelped as she squirted her pleasure all over him. It felt so tight deep down inside her, and as she contracted over him with waves of pleasure; it shot through him and in to her, leaving them both breathless.

Constellina handed the Prince the pole; it was still sodden from Aurora's juices. The Prince licked it up and down. He placed it against the edge of The Pixie's vagina and pulled it apart with the tip of his finger and his penis. He exerted a firm pressure and the pole went plunging in to the Pixie's tiny hole, and she yelped and sat down on them harder. She bounced furiously up and down on the Prince and the pole, wanting to feel every bit of them inside her. She'd never been filled like this before, and the feeling was so intense it was overwhelming. She couldn't help but keep bouncing on the Prince as he thrust himself and the pole in and out of her over and over, bringing her to orgasm after orgasm. She felt her hole being filling with pleasure flowing from her depths as the Prince and the pole moved against her writhing womanhood. She felt the Prince swell further and throb against her pulsating vagina. He felt his excitement peak and the warm release rush out of him, and he cried out with pleasure. She clenched over him as he finished, experiencing another intense multiple orgasm.

"My Prince, I would like the honor of using this tool on our beautiful maidens here, please, if you will." The Prince handed the pole to the elf-man. Constellina was already in front of him and reached up to wrap her arms behind his neck.

"No need to be gentle good sir, I am willing," she smiled up at him. He rose immediately, and she maneuvered herself so that he slid inside her with little resistance. She spread her legs to accommodate for him and let out a sigh as he entered her. He pulled her down on to him and smiled as he watched her engulf all of him. He pulled back and placed the pole next to his penis against the entrance of her vagina. He moved his penis aside slightly and pressed the edge of the pole in to her against his penis. The pole was soaked with several lubricants and began to slide in to her against his penis. As he continued pushing it slowly in to her, she spread her legs wider to accommodate for her expanding orifice. She felt herself clench harder over the pole as it fought to spread her wider. Just as the elf thought he had reached as far as he could go in to her, Constellina bent over, placed her hands in front of her and shoved herself back over on to them both. The elf gasped in shock and Constellina gasped with pleasure as she felt fully filled. The elf-man didn't hesitate and thrust the pole and himself in and out of Constellina over and over. She pushed back against him as the feelings of pleasure increased inside her. The pixie was unable to resist and flew over to assist Constellina to a massive climax as the elf-man felt the release leave him as he finished inside of her. Meanwhile, the Prince had Aurora bent over on all fours and pounded himself and her to a fast and furious finish.

The men withdrew when they finished and maneuvered themselves so they were surrounded by the three women. The elf-man, still holding the pole, plunged it in and up in to the pixie's depths. She howled and bounced herself up and down on it, using the fluttering effects of her wings to tickle the tips of the elfin women's clitorises. The Prince and the elf-man watched the elves getting more aroused. They approached them from behind and slid their arms around them, cupping their breasts, and placed their penises between their dripping thighs. The elves guided them so they slid inside and released a unanimous moan of pleasure as they thrust in and out of them until they all reached an intense and vocal climax.

"Come, we must continue on our way; the Kingdom is less than half a day's travel from here," Constellina announced as they caught their breath. Both of the elfin maidens were very aware of the Prince's fragile state and that it was crucial to reach the Kingdom before nightfall if they wished to avoid another dangerous encounter. The rest of them rose to their feet, and the pixie continued to flutter skywards. Constellina strode ahead towards the end of their eventful travels.

As they reached the castle gates, they were greeted with triumphant cheers and huge sighs of relief to learn of the Prince's safety. They had arrived just in time, as tonight the full moon would rise once again, and the Prince would hide in darkness.

That night, Constellina and Aurora visited him as they had promised, breaching the guards and security measures with ease. Their elfin stealth far surpassed that of any humans. As they entered the Prince's dungeon chamber, the moonlight revealed itself and he transformed once again before them. They could tell he knew why they were there, for as he transformed his massive member grew and glowed red before them amongst the rest of the darkness. Satisfied but still feeling ripe and ready, the elfin maids pressed their naked bodies against the walls, face first. They both jutted their beautiful behinds out and upwards towards the werewolf. They reached down and caressed their clitorises, sighing with pleasure as the werewolf continued to approach. They then turned and reached towards each other and placed their hands on each others' genitals and kissed with their tongues all over their faces. The wolf paused and looked down at himself. He reached for his throbbing member with his tongue and began to lick up and down his hot red shaft. The elves thrust their buttocks out further at him as they brought each other to orgasm.

The wolf moved forward on all fours, his nose was close enough for them to hear his breath. He looked to Aurora, then Constellina, back to Aurora, and then he reached forward with his tongue and touched Constellina. She gasped as she felt the moist touch stimulate waves of pleasure from deep within her. She pushed further back on to the wolf as she felt his huge canine tongue slide deep inside of her. She moaned a response as she felt him reach down in to her depths as far as he could go and tickle her insides. He slid his tongue in and out of her as he felt her grow wetter and clench over him.

Constellina reached over to Aurora and slid two fingers deep inside her while she rubbed her clitoris with the other. She felt Aurora drip all over her as she moaned with pleasure. Aurora lifted her buttocks up and down as she clenched over Constellina's fingers as they slid in and out of her with ease, Constellina added another finger, and another. She was penetrating Aurora with four of her fingers with ease. Aurora felt herself growing closer to climax. Just as she felt she was going to come, she felt Constellina's four fingers pull out of her and the werewolf's hot wet tongue replace them. He brought Aurora to a drenched and screaming orgasm as he stroked over the bottom of her depths and moved his tongue vigorously inside her as he felt her clench over him.

The wolf pulled his tongue out of Aurora's genitals, rose up on his hind legs and slammed himself against Constellina. Her legs spread as wide as they could go but still only his tip had penetrated her. She pushed back against him and felt him thrust the rest of himself inside of her and let out a cry of pleasure as she engulfed him, he howled. He pressed himself against her, and she felt his hot breath in her ear and his shaggy fur against her skin as he pounded her to an orgasmic oblivion. The werewolf howled as he released his pleasure deep inside her. He withdrew and immediately turned to Constellina. She felt him press against her but miss, his hot and throbbing penis slid under her, and she gasped as she felt it slide over her clitoris. He pulled back, aimed and slammed it deep inside her. She pushed back against him until she had engulfed him entirely. She let out an orgasmic cry as her walls contracted and gushed all over the werewolf's penis. The wolf leaned all the way over Constellina, until he had her bent over on to all fours, the top of her back against the wall as she tucked her head underneath herself. He thrust himself in and out of her in true doggy-style; she could feel her excitement rise with each stroke in and out, and she was almost there.

She felt Aurora slide herself underneath her and looked down to be greeted by her gaping wet vagina and swollen and expectant clitoris. As she drank in the sight of her partner's aroused genitals, she felt Aurora lick her clitoris with her tongue, and she reached orgasm immediately and clenched over the werewolf, who increased the force of his thrusts. Constellina plunged her face in to Aurora's genitalia a few times but was soon overwhelmed by her orgasmic feelings. She threw her head back and vocalized her pleasure for the entire

Kingdom to hear. The werewolf took it upon himself to reach for Aurora's genitals with his enormous canine tongue. She moaned as she felt it slide over and in to her. He increased his pace and brought her to climax as Constellina clenched harder and faster over his penis. The werewolf howled his triumph as Constellina came and brought him to another almighty climax. He slammed her hard in to the wall, and she slammed herself back against him. He was so far in to her now they appeared to be one.

The Prince transformed back in to his human form as he withdrew from her. They all lay down on the huge bed in the corner of the elaborate dungeon room and slept until dawn.

ABOUT THE AUTHOR

Readers: I want to expand a few of the stories to see where the characters can be explored further. If there are any of the stories that you would like to read more about again, I'd love to hear from you!

Visit my blog at
http://www.mackenzieharnden.com

Join my newsletter for free exclusive previews
http://www.mackenzieharnden.com/in

Follow me on Twitter at
http://www.twitter.com/mckenzieharnden

Like my page on Facebook at
http://www.facebook.com/mackenzieharnden

Discover my books at major ebook retailers everywhere.